东方智慧丛书　The Wisdom of the East Series

学术顾问：张葆全　　　　　　　Academic Adviser: Zhang Baoquan
主　　编：汤文辉　刘志强　　　Editors-in-Chief: Tang Wenhui　Liu Zhiqiang

编辑委员会：　　　　　　　　　Editorial Board
主　任：虞劲松　郭玉贤　　　　Directors: Yu Jingsong　Guo Yuxian
　　　　尤晓澍　　　　　　　　　　　　　You Xiaoshu
委　员：才学娟　王　专　　　　Members: Cai Xuejuan　Wang Zhuan
　　　　王　燕　杨远义　　　　　　　　　Wang Yan　Yang Yuanyi
　　　　陈丕武　施　萍　　　　　　　　　Chen Piwu　Shi Ping
　　　　梁嗣辰　梁鑫磊　　　　　　　　　Liang Sichen　Liang Xinlei
　　　　邹旭勇　原野菁　　　　　　　　　Zou Xuyong　Yuan Yejing

翻译委员会：　　　　　　　　　Committee of Translators
主　任：黎巧萍　刘志强　　　　Directors: Li Qiaoping　Liu Zhiqiang
　　　　覃秀红　　　　　　　　　　　　　Qin Xiuhong
委　员：王海玲　吴思远　　　　Members: Wang Hailing　Wu Siyuan
　　　　沈　菲　张　蔚　　　　　　　　　Shen Fei　Zhang Wei
　　　　欧江玲　徐明月　　　　　　　　　Ou Jiangling　Xu Mingyue
　　　　谈　笑　陶　红　　　　　　　　　Tan Xiao　Tao Hong
　　　　黄兴球　覃海伦　　　　　　　　　Huang Xingqiu　Qin Hailun
　　　　韩艳妍　　　　　　　　　　　　　Han Yanyan

美术委员会：　　　　　　　　　Committee of Art Editors
主　任：柴万里　尹　红　　　　Directors: Qi Wanli　Yin Hong
委　员：卫阳虹　王雪峰　　　　Members: Wei Yanghong　Wang Xuefeng
　　　　吕　鹏　刘　荣　　　　　　　　　Lü Peng　Liu Rong
　　　　关婷月　郑振铭　　　　　　　　　Guan Tingyue　Zheng Zhenming
　　　　俞　崧　陶朝来　　　　　　　　　Yu Song　Tao Chaolai
　　　　黄建福　蓝学会　　　　　　　　　Huang Jianfu　Lan Xuehui
　　　　戴孟云　　　　　　　　　　　　　Dai Mengyun

The Wisdom of the East Series
东方智慧丛书
Editors-in-Chief: Tang Wenhui　Liu Zhiqiang
主编：汤文辉　刘志强
Academic Adviser: Zhang Baoquan
学术顾问：张葆全

Chinese-English
汉　英　对　照

Song Lyrics (Selections)
宋词选译

Compiled and Commented by Shi Ping
选释：施萍
Proofread by Zhang Baoquan
中文审读：张葆全
Translated by Wu Siyuan
翻译：吴思远
Illustrated by Li Zhenying
绘图：李贞莹

·桂林 Guilin·
GUANGXI NORMAL UNIVERSITY PRESS
广西师范大学出版社

© 2023 by Guangxi Normal University Press.
All rights reserved.

图书在版编目（CIP）数据

宋词选译：汉文、英文 / 施萍选释；吴思远译；李贞莹绘. --桂林：广西师范大学出版社，2023.3
（东方智慧丛书 / 汤文辉等主编）
ISBN 978-7-5598-5855-9

Ⅰ.①宋… Ⅱ.①施… ②吴… ③李… Ⅲ.①宋词－诗歌欣赏－汉、英 Ⅳ.①I207.23

中国国家版本馆 CIP 数据核字（2023）第 038303 号

广西师范大学出版社出版发行

（广西桂林市五里店路 9 号　邮政编码：541004
　网址：http://www.bbtpress.com）

出版人：黄轩庄
全国新华书店经销
广西广大印务有限责任公司印刷
（桂林市临桂区秧塘工业园西城大道北侧广西师范大学出版社集团有限公司创意产业园内　邮政编码：541199）
开本：880 mm × 1 240 mm　1/32
印张：8.5　　字数：180 千　　图：50 幅
2023 年 3 月第 1 版　　2023 年 3 月第 1 次印刷
定价：78.00 元

如发现印装质量问题，影响阅读，请与出版社发行部门联系调换。

总　序

　　文化交流对人类社会的存在与发展至关重要。季羡林先生曾指出，文化交流是推动人类社会前进的主要动力之一，文化一旦产生，就必然交流，这种交流是任何力量也阻挡不住的。由于文化交流，世界各民族的文化才能互相补充，共同发展，才能形成今天世界上万紫千红的文化繁荣现象。[1]

　　中国与东盟国家的文化交流亦然，并且具有得天独厚的优势。首先，中国与东盟许多国家地理相接，山水相连，不少民族之间普遍存在着跨居、通婚现象，这为文化交流奠定了良好的地理与人文基础。其次，古代中国与世界其他国家建立起的"海上丝绸之路"为中国与东盟国家的经济、文化交流创造了有利的交通条件。

　　中国与东盟诸多使用不同语言文字的民族进行思想与文化对话，

---

[1] 季羡林：《文化的冲突与融合·序》，载张岱年、汤一介等《文化的冲突与融合》，北京大学出版社，1997年，第2页。

自然离不开翻译。翻译活动一般又分为口译和笔译两类。有史记载的中国与东盟之间的口译活动可以追溯至西周时期,但笔译活动则出现在明代,至今已逾五百年的历史。

在过去五百年的历史长河中,东盟国家大量地译介了中国的文化作品,其中不少已经融入本国的文化中去。中国译介东盟国家的作品也不在少数。以文字为载体的相互译介活动,更利于文化的传承与发展,把中国与东盟国家的文化交流推上了更高的层次。

2013年9月,国务院总理李克强在广西南宁举行的第十届中国—东盟博览会开幕式上发表主旨演讲时指出,中国与东盟携手开创了合作的"黄金十年"。他呼吁中国与东盟百尺竿头更进一步,创造新的"钻石十年"。2013年10月,习近平总书记在周边外交工作座谈会上强调要对外介绍好我国的内外方针政策,讲好中国故事,传播好中国声音,把中国梦同周边各国人民过上美好生活的愿望、同地区发展前景对接起来,让命运共同体意识在周边国家落地生根。于是,把中华文化的经典译介至东盟国家,不仅具有重要的历史意义,同时还蕴含着浓厚的时代气息。

所谓交流,自然包括"迎来送往",《礼记》有言:"往而不来,非礼也;来而不往,亦非礼也。"中国与东盟国家一样,既翻译和引进外国的优秀文化,同时也把本国文化的精髓部分推介出去。作为中国最具人文思想的出版社之一——广西师范大学出版社构想了《东方智慧丛书》,并付诸实践,不仅是中国翻译学界、人文学界的大事,更是中国与东盟进行良好沟通、增进相互了解的必然选择。广东外语外贸大学和广西民族大学作为翻译工作的主要承担方,都是国家外语非通用语种本科人才培养基地,拥有东盟语言文字的翻译优势。三个单位的合作将能够擦出更多的火花,向东盟国家更好地传播中华文化。

联合国教科文组织的官员认为,"文化交流是新的全球化现象"。[1]我们希望顺应这一历史潮流与时代趋势,做一点力所能及的事。

是为序。

刘志强

2015年1月25日

---

[1]《联合国教科文组织文化政策与跨文化对话司司长卡特瑞娜·斯泰诺的致辞》,载《世界文化的东亚视角》,北京大学出版社,2004年,第3页。

Preface to The Wisdom of the East Series

Cultural exchanges are of significant importance to the existence and development of human society. Mr. Ji Xianlin once pointed out that cultural exchange was one of the major driving forces for the progress of human society. It is inevitable that communications and exchanges will occur among different cultures. As a result, the interaction and mutual enrichment of cultures contribute to the formation of a diversified world featured by cultural prosperity.[1]

The cultural exchange between China and ASEAN countries, in the trend of mutual communication and interaction, also boasts of its own unique strengths. First of all, China borders many ASEAN countries both by land and by sea, and intermarriage and transnational settlement are common, all of which lay a solid foundation for cultural exchanges. In addition, the "Maritime Silk

---

[1] Ji Xianlin, "Preface to Cultural Conflicts and Integration", in *Cultural Conflicts and Integration*, edited by Zhang Dainian, Tang Yijie, et al. Beijing: Beijing University Press, 1997, p.2.

Road" developed by ancient China and other countries has helped pave the way to a smooth economic and cultural exchange between China and ASEAN countries.

People from China and ASEAN countries use different languages. Thus, to conduct a successful dialogue in the cultural field requires the involvement of translation and oral interpretation. Historical records show that the oral interpretation among people of China and ASEAN can be dated back to the Western Zhou Dynasty (1122-771 B.C.). It is also known that translation started to boom in the Ming Dynasty, which was five hundred years ago.

In the past five hundred years, a large number of Chinese cultural works were translated into many languages of ASEAN countries and many of them have been integrated into their local cultures. China has also translated a lot of works of ASEAN countries. Translation is beneficial to inheritance and development of culture and upgrades the cultural exchanges between China and ASEAN to a higher level.

As Mr. Li Keqiang, Premier of the State Council of the People's Republic of China, pointed out in his speech at the opening ceremony of the 10th China-ASEAN Expo held in Nanning in September, 2013, China and ASEAN jointly created "10 golden years" of cooperation. And he called on both sides to upgrade their cooperation to a new level by creating "10 diamond years". In October, 2013, General Secretary Xi Jinping emphasized, in a meeting with Chinese diplomats, the importance of introducing China's domestic and foreign policies to other countries and regions, and making Chinese voice heard in the world. Xi also pointed out that "Chinese Dream" should be connected with her neighboring countries' dream of a better life and with the development prospect of those countries so as to build up a community of shared destiny. Against such a backdrop, it's of both historical and current significance to translate Chinese classics and introduce them to ASEAN countries.

Exchanges are reciprocal. According to *The Book of Rites*, behaviors that do not reciprocate are not consistent with rites. Like ASEAN countries, China has had excellent foreign cultural works translated and introduced domestically, and also translated and introduced to the outside world the essence of local culture and thoughts. Guangxi Normal University Press, one of the top presses in China that focus on enhancing the influence of the humanities, made the decision to publish *The Wisdom of the East Series*. It is not only a big event in Chinese academia, but also a necessary choice for China and ASEAN to communicate with each other and enhance mutual understanding. Guangdong University of Foreign Studies, and Guangxi University for Nationalities, the main undertakers of the translation project, are both national non-universal languages training bases for undergraduates and boast strengths of ASEAN languages. Cooperation between the two universities and the press will surely facilitate dissemination of traditional Chinese culture to ASEAN countries.

UNESCO officials hold the belief that cultural exchange is a new phenomenon of globalization.[1] We hope that our efforts could breathe the spirit of this historical momentum and help ASEAN countries understand Chinese culture better.

Liu Zhiqiang
January 25, 2015

---

[1] "Speech of Katerina stenou, Director of Division of Cultural Policies and Intercultural Dialogue", from *East Asia's View on World Culture*. Beijing: Beijing University Press, 2004, p.3.

宋词选译
Song Lyrics (Selections)

前 言

词，又称诗余，曲子词，长短句，是一种起源于隋唐、兴盛于宋、伴随着燕乐（宫廷中饮宴时供娱乐欣赏的歌舞音乐，即宴乐）而兴起的、句式参差不齐的新体诗歌，在宋代是一种盛行的文学样式。

在篇幅、句式、平仄、用韵上，词和格律诗一样有较为严格的规定。但词也有自己的一些体裁特点。

首先，词有词调。词调是指写词时所依据的乐谱，是总结词的句法、平仄等形成的一种固定的格式，每种格式都有一个词牌名，如"鹧鸪天""卜算子""蝶恋花"等。作词是在固定的格式下对词的内容进行填充，所以又叫填词。

其次，词有分片。除了一些小令是"单调"之外，多数词作都是"双调"词，即有分片，称为"上片""下片"，或者"上阕""下阕"，有的甚至有"三叠""四叠"。片与片之间要有词意上的连贯性。

最后，词的用韵也与诗歌有所不同，主要根据各词调的不同，来确定不同的用韵，有较强的变化。

词产生于民间,发现于敦煌的《敦煌曲子词》抄本,较详细地证明了这一点。中唐以后,刘禹锡、张志和等文人才加入了词的创作队伍。但所作多为《渔歌子》《忆江南》等小令,数量也较少。及至晚唐,词的创作有了较大的发展,出现了以温庭筠、韦庄等为代表的"花间派"(见后蜀赵崇祚所编《花间集》),以男女相恋、悲欢离合为主题,风格绮丽婉约。而区别于后蜀"花间派"的南唐后主李煜,则运用白描的手法,将身世之感、亡国之哀融入词作中,写出了大量艺术水平较高的作品,将词的发展推上一个新的境界。

北宋前期,词在题材风格上依然延续晚唐五代。欧阳修、晏殊、晏几道等人均生活在北宋太平时期,词作大多反映士大夫阶层的闲适生活,形式上仍以篇幅短小的小令居多。柳永是北宋前期词坛最有影响力的词人,他创作了大量不同于小令的、依照慢调所填写的调长拍缓的词,即慢词,扩大了词的容量和表现能力。同时,作为一个不得志的文人,柳永常常出没于教坊乐肆,对当时的市民生活有着相当深入的了解,再加上他有相当高的音乐素养,所以创作出了一大批广泛流传的词作,"凡有井水处,皆能歌柳词"(南宋叶梦得《避暑录话》)。

北宋后期,词作的内容开始扩大,风格上也有了较大的变化。词的创作渐渐打破了原先只写艳情、用语绮丽的局面,开始出现了像苏轼这样的革新者。在题材方面,苏轼将怀古、咏史、咏物、记梦、酬赠等,均写入词中,扩大了词的描写内容;在风格方面,苏词豪迈奔放,潇洒不羁,《念奴娇·赤壁怀古》《江城子·密州出猎》等均写出了阔大的气象。同时,苏轼对词作为一种独立文体的社会地位的提高也做出了贡献。从苏轼开始,词不再只是音乐的附属品,而是同诗一样,作为一种独立的文体开始表达思想、抒发情感。而与苏轼同时期的周邦彦,则被称为"集大成"者,他上承晏(殊、几道)、柳(永),下开姜(夔)、张(炎),通音律、工慢词,作词章法缜密,对后世有很大的影响。这个时期，还有一位不可忽视的词人，李清照。她的词善用白描，语言清丽婉约，同时十分注重音乐乐律的和谐。李清照提出词"别是一家"，不可与诗相混。

到了南宋，反映民族矛盾的主题占据了较重要的地位。张元幹、张孝祥、陆游、辛弃疾等，均有反映斗争题材的作品。其中，尤以辛弃疾的成就最高。辛词在风格上承袭苏词，词风慷慨激昂；在形式上，"以文为词"，将经、史、子、集中的书面用语融入自己的词作当中，使词更具表现力和生命力。与陆游、辛弃疾等慷慨悲歌的词人相对应的是南宋词坛的另一派。其中以姜夔、张炎等为代表，词风雅正清空，内容多为描写士大夫阶层的闲适生活。南宋后期，国势衰微，姜、张等人的词已不能表达对时事的看法，疏泄内心情绪，此时出现的刘克庄、刘辰翁、文天祥等就继承了苏、辛的豪放传统，写出了大量慷慨悲凉的词作。

到了元朝，写词多模仿前人，少有创新，词这种体裁也渐渐衰落。到了清代，词一度"中兴"，不再只是"倚声"的小道，在表现社会现实方面显示了其强大的功力。有清一代，出现了纳兰性德、朱彝尊、龚自珍等大家，也出现了诸多的流派，如以陈维崧为代表的阳羡派，以张惠言为代表的常州派等。在当代，词这种文体依然深受大众喜爱，时见有借词来抒心中之意者。

一代有一代之文学，有宋一代，词的创作达到了极高的水平，优秀的词作也不胜枚举。本书在蔡义江《宋词三百首》、胡云翼《宋词选》、中国社会科学院文学研究所《唐宋词选》等选本的基础上精选宋词50首，配以释文和解析，希望读者朋友们能从中领略宋词之美。

Preface

The Song lyrics, or *ci* poetry, are known as *shiyu* (that which is beside poetry), or *changduanju* (line of irregular lengths). Derived from Tang poetry, this new poetic form of literature was developed with the emergence of banquet music, and had its heyday in Song dynasty.

To compose either poetry or lyrics, there are many strict requirements in terms of length, stanzas, tonal and rhythmic patterns, etc. But lyrics have certain distinctive features.

Firstly, there is a tune pattern. It refers to a fixed format in accordance with the melody. And each format is associated with a tune title, for instance, "Partridge Sky," "Divination," "Butterflies Linger with Flowers," etc. To compose a lyric song is to fill in the fixed format with the right words, so lyric composition is also called "lyric-filling."

Secondly, there are different stanzas. Except for some *xiaoling* (the poetic form that is short in length and fast in tempo), Song lyrics are mostly consisted of two stanzas, and some of them are even with three or four stanzas. Between two stanzas, semantic coherence must be maintained.

Lastly, the rhythmic requirements for lyrics are not the same as those for composing poetry. According to tune titles, there will be uniquely different rhythms.

Song lyrics were developed from popular songs and folk culture, and the preserved manuscript *Song Lyrics of Dunhuang* is a good case in point. Since the Mid-Tang (766—835) period, famous literati such as Liu Yuxi (772—842) and Zhang Zhihe (730—810) joined the group of lyric writers. But what they wrote are only a small number of *xiaoling*, such as "Fishermen's Song" and "Recollection of the Southern Land." The Late-Tang (836—907) period witnessed a great development in the composition of lyrics. There appeared a "Flowery School," with Wen Tingyun (812—870) and Wei Zhuang (836—910) as its representative poets. Their works are mainly about love, reunion and separation, with an elegant and restrained style. In contrast, the poet Li Yu (937—978) was famous for his works that focus on vicissitude of life and lamentation on the downfall of his country. He had composed a large number of songs in plain language and with high literary value. His works has brought the lyrics to a higher level.

Carrying on the themes and styles formed in the Late-Tang and Five Dynasties and Ten Kingdoms (907—960) periods, lyric songs continued to develop in the early period of Northern Song (960—1127) dynasty. Well known writers, like Ouyang Xiu (1007—1072), Yan Shu (991—1055), and Yan Jidao (1038—1110), all lived in a peaceful period, therefore, their works often reflected the leisure life of the scholar-official class, and were mostly in the format of *xiaoling*. During this period, the most influential lyrics poet, Liu Yong (987—1053), completed plenty of songs that were different from *xiaoling*. These songs were in long poetic form and slow tempo, which allowed more room for characters and representations. As an unfulfilled scholar, Liu Yong was a regular visitor of brothels and entertainment venues, thus he was quite familiar with the urban culture. In addition, he had great expertise on music. Hence, he was able to produce a great number of popular lyric songs. According to Ye Mengde (1077—1148)'s *Records of Conversations While Escaping Summer Heat*, "where there is a well, there will be the lyric songs by Liu Yong singing around".

In the late period of the Northern Song, there were changes both in content and in style. The lyrics were no longer limited to romantic love and flowery language. Innovators such as Su Shi (1037—1101) began to appear. In terms of the topics, Su wrote about the thoughts on past and history, odes to subjects, dreams, and reciprocating songs, all of which greatly extended the scope of content in lyrics. In terms of the styles, Su's lyrics were featured by a strong sense of boldness, broadness and unrestrained freedom, for example, "Remembering the Pretty Maid" (Thoughts on the Past at Red Cliff) and "River Town" (Hunting at Mizhou). At the same time, Su Shi made contribution to the establishment of Song lyrics as an independent genre of Chinese literature. Thanks to Su's efforts, lyrics were not just passively affiliated with tunes, but became more independent and inclusive to convey thoughts and feelings of the writers. The works of Zhou Bangyan (1057—1121),

Su Shi's contemporary writer, were extremely influential. He was an expert in music, a master of lyrics in slow tempo, and a practitioner of strict composition requirements. He inherited the fine tradition and broke new ground for future. Before him, there were Yan Shu and Liu Yong, and after him, there were Jiang Kui (1154—1221) and Zhang Yan (1248—1320). There was another poet who must not be overlooked: Li Qingzhao (1084—1155). Her plain language brought an elegant taste and restrained style to the readers, and matched harmoniously the tunes of the songs. She pointed out that lyrics should be "an independent genre of literature," a literary form that differs from poetry.

In the Southern Song (1127—1279) dynasty, the theme that reflected ethnic conflicts occupied an important place in the development of lyrics. Zhang Yuangan (1091—1161), Zhang Xiaoxiang (1132—1170), Lu You (1125—1210), Xin Qiji (1140—1207) and others all wrote works concerning battles. Among them, Xin Qiji was the highest in poetic achievement. Carrying on the style of Su Shi's lyrics, Xin's works were characterized by enthusiastic patriotism. Due to his employment of written language from Confucian classics, historical documents, philosophical works, and literary collections, Xin's works were more expressive and vivid. There was another group of lyrics writers with Jiang Kui and Zhang Yan as the representatives. Contrary to Lu and Xin, their works were more tasteful and concerned with leisure life of the scholar officials. But in the late period of the Southern Song, the political situation became worse, and to comment on the national affairs and channel the depressed feelings, such a style seemed to be insufficient. Naturally, there appeared Liu Kezhuang (1187—1269), Liu Chenweng (1233—

1297), and Wen Tianxiang (1236—1283), who inherited the tradition of Su and Xin's works, and left plenty of lyric songs with a passionate tone.

In Yuan (1271—1368) dynasty, those who wrote lyrics could rarely be called innovative poets, for they basically followed their predecessors. Hence, this literary genre came to be less significant. In Qing (1644—1911) dynasty, there appeared a phase of revival. Lyrics were not just an insignificant literary form attached to tunes, for they were playing a critical role in representing social realities. Influential poets and schools abounded in this period: Nalan Xingde (1655—1685), Zhu Yizun (1629—1709), Gong Zizhen (1792—1841), Yangxian School, and Changzhou School, etc. Even nowadays, lyrics are still very popular among the general public, and there are many people who often employ lyrics to express their own feelings.

In Chinese literary history, every dynasty has its own representative literary. In Song dynasty, a large number of excellent lyrics were produced with high aesthetic and literary values. Based on *Three Hundred Song Lyrics* edited by Cai Yijiang, *Selections of Song Lyrics* edited by Hu Yunyi, and *Selections of Tang and Song Lyrics* edited by Literature Research Institute of Chinese Academy of Social Science, this present volume collects fifty Song lyrics, and provides a commentary for each lyric song. It is our hope that readers could get a glimpse of the beauty in Song lyrics.

目 录

1. 《玉楼春·城上风光莺语乱》 钱惟演 ………………… 2
2. 《渔家傲·塞下秋来风景异》 范仲淹 ………………… 6
3. 《苏幕遮·碧云天》 范仲淹 ……………………………… 12
4. 《天仙子·水调数声持酒听》 张先 …………………… 18
5. 《浣溪沙·一曲新词酒一杯》 晏殊 …………………… 24
6. 《蝶恋花·槛菊愁烟兰泣露》 晏殊 …………………… 28
7. 《破阵子·燕子来时新社》 晏殊 ……………………… 32
8. 《玉楼春·东城渐觉风光好》 宋祁 …………………… 36
9. 《踏莎行·候馆梅残》 欧阳修 ………………………… 40

Contents

1. "Jade Tower in Spring" (Chirps of orioles are heard among the glorious scenery in the town)　by Qian Weiyan ·············· 3
2. "Pride of the Fishermen" (When autumn comes, the scenery becomes different in the border area)　by Fan Zhongyan ·············· 7
3. "Screened by Southern Curtain" (The sky is blue with clouds)　by Fan Zhongyan ·············· 13
4. "Heavenly Fairy" (With a wine cup in hand, I listen to the tune of Water Melody)　by Zhang Xian ·············· 19
5. "Sand at Silk Washing Stream" (A song filled with new words and a cup of wine)　by Yan Shu ·············· 25
6. "Butterflies Linger with Flowers" (Beside the balustrade, chrysanthemums are sad in mist and orchids are shedding tears of dew)　by Yan Shu ··· 29
7. "Breaking the Formation" (When the swallows return, it is the New Communal Day)　by Yan Shu ·············· 33
8. "Spring in Jade Tower" (The scenery in the eastern city seems gradually to be fine)　by Song Qi ·············· 37
9. "Treading on Grass" (Around the inn, the plums are withered)　by Ouyang Xiu ·············· 41

10.《浪淘沙·把酒祝东风》　　欧阳修 ················· 44

11.《蝶恋花·庭院深深深几许》　　欧阳修 ············ 48

12.《雨霖铃·寒蝉凄切》　柳永 ······················· 52

13.《望海潮·东南形胜》　柳永 ······················· 58

14.《八声甘州·对潇潇暮雨洒江天》　　柳永 ·········· 64

15.《蝶恋花·伫倚危楼风细细》　　柳永 ··············· 70

16.《桂枝香·登临送目》　王安石 ····················· 74

17.《临江仙·梦后楼台高锁》　　晏几道 ··············· 80

18.《鹧鸪天·彩袖殷勤捧玉钟》　　晏几道 ············ 84

19.《水调歌头·明月几时有》　　苏轼 ················· 88

20.《江城子·十年生死两茫茫》　　苏轼 ··············· 94

21.《念奴娇·大江东去》　苏轼 ······················· 98

22.《定风波·莫听穿林打叶声》　　苏轼 ·············· 104

23.《卜算子·缺月挂疏桐》　苏轼 ···················· 108

10. "Waves Dredging Sand" (Holding a wine cup, I drink a toast to eastern wind) by Ouyang Xiu ·· 45
11. "Butterflies Linger over Flowers" (So deep is the courtyard, but how deep is it?) by Ouyang Xiu ·· 49
12. "Bells Ringing in the Rain" (Cold cicadas are chirping dolefully) by Liu Yong ·· 53
13. "Seeing Sea Tide" (Located in the southeast) by Liu Yong ············ 59
14. "Ganzhou Melody of Eight Rhymes" (I face the pattering rain in the evening pouring from river sky) by Liu Yong ·· 65
15. "Butterflies Linger with Flowers" (In light and soft breeze, I lean against the balustrade on a high tower) by Liu Yong ·· 71
16. "Fragrance of Cinnamon Twigs" (I make a climb to cast my eyes afar) by Wang Anshi ·· 75
17. "Immortal at Riverside" (I wake up from a dream, and the high tower is locked) by Yan Jidao ·· 81
18. "Partridge Sky" (The colorful sleeves cordially serve the jade bells) by Yan Jidao ·· 85
19. "Prelude to Water Melody" (How long will the bright moon appear) by Su Shi ·· 89
20. "River Town" (For ten years, the living and the dead are both in ignorance of each other) by Su Shi ·· 95
21. "Charm of a Maiden Singer" (The great river flows to the east) by Su Shi ·· 99
22. "Calm the Waves" (Do not listen to the rain that rustles the woods and beats against the leaves) by Su Shi ·· 105
23. "Divination" (The waning moon hangs over the sparse wutong tree) by Su Shi ·· 109

24.《清平乐·春归何处》　黄庭坚 ················ 112

25.《鹊桥仙·纤云弄巧》　秦观 ·················· 116

26.《踏莎行·雾失楼台》　秦观 ·················· 120

27.《青玉案·凌波不过横塘路》　贺铸 ············ 124

28.《鹧鸪天·重过阊门万事非》　贺铸 ············ 130

29.《卜算子·水是眼波横》　王观 ················ 134

30.《卜算子·我住长江头》　李之仪 ·············· 138

31.《苏幕遮·燎沉香》　周邦彦 ·················· 142

32.《醉花阴·薄雾浓云愁永昼》　李清照 ·········· 146

33.《如梦令·常记溪亭日暮》　李清照 ············ 150

34.《如梦令·昨夜疏雨风骤》　李清照 ············ 154

35.《声声慢·寻寻觅觅》　李清照 ················ 158

36.《鹧鸪天·我是清都山水郎》　朱敦儒 ·········· 164

37.《贺新郎·梦绕神州路》　张元幹 ·············· 168

38.《小重山·昨夜寒蛩不住鸣》　岳飞 ············ 174

24. "Pure Serene Music" (Where has spring gone?) by Huang Tingjian ··· 113
25. "Magpie Bridge Immortal" (Slender clouds display delicate shapes)
    by Qin Guan ·· 117
26. "Treading on Grass" (Towers and terraces are lost in mist)
    by Qin Guan ·· 121
27. "Green Jade Table" (Her graceful steps are not across the Road of
    Horizontal Pond) by He Zhu ·· 125
28. "Partridge Sky" (I pass Chang Gate again, but everything is different)
    by He Zhu ·· 131
29. "Divination" (The waters are the waves across the eyes)
    by Wang Guan ·· 135
30. "Divination" (I live upstream of the Yangtze) by Li Zhiyi ············· 139
31. "Screened by Southern Curtain" (Burning the eaglewood incense)
    by Zhou Bangyan ·· 143
32. "Intoxicated in Flowers Shade" (Light mists, dense clouds, and a long
    day in melancholy.) by Li Qingzhao ·· 147
33. "A Dream-like Song" (I often recall the dusk at the pavilion by a stream)
    by Li Qingzhao ··· 151
34. "A Dream-like Song" (Last night, the rain was light and the wind was
    rapid) by Li Qingzhao ·· 155
35. "Adagio of Resonance" (Seeking and searching) by Li Qingzhao ······ 159
36. "Partridge Sky" (I am the officer of mountain and river in clear capital)
    by Zhu Dunru ··· 165
37. "Congratulations to the Groom" (In dreams, I wander around the paths
    of the Divine Land.) by Zhang Yuangan ································· 169
38. "Manifold Little Hill" (Last night the autumn crickets chirped
    incessantly) by Yue Fei ·· 175

39.《钗头凤·红酥手》　　陆游 ·················· 178

40.《卜算子·驿外断桥边》　　陆游 ·············· 184

41.《六州歌头·长淮望断》　　张孝祥 ············· 188

42.《西江月·明月别枝惊鹊》　　辛弃疾 ············ 194

43.《破阵子·醉里挑灯看剑》　　辛弃疾 ············ 198

44.《永遇乐·千古江山》　　辛弃疾 ··············· 202

45.《青玉案·东风夜放花千树》　　辛弃疾 ·········· 208

46.《扬州慢·淮左名都》　　姜夔 ················ 212

47.《风入松·听风听雨过清明》　　吴文英 ·········· 218

48.《眉妩·渐新痕悬柳》　　王沂孙 ··············· 222

49.《一剪梅·一片春愁待酒浇》　　蒋捷 ············ 228

50.《高阳台·接叶巢莺》　　张炎 ················ 232

39. "Phoenix Hairpin" (Pink tender hands)   by Lu You ·················· 179
40. "Divination" (Outside the post house, and beside the broken bridge) by Lu You ··· 185
41. "Preludes to the Songs of Six States" (I look at the long Huai River in distance until it vanishes)   by Zhang Xiaoxiang ······················ 189
42. "Western River Moon" (A bright moon over yonder branches startles the magpies)   by Xin Qiji ··· 195
43. "Breaking the Formation" (In drunkenness, I trim the lamp wick to see the sword)   by Xin Qiji ··· 199
44. "Forever in Happiness" (Among rivers and mountains since the ancient times)   by Xin Qiji ··· 203
45. "Green Jade Table" (Eastern wind at night blows the flowers of a thousand trees)   by Xin Qiji ··· 209
46. "Yangzhou Adagio" (In this famed town, east of the Huai River) by Jiang Kui ··· 213
47. "Wind through Pines" (Hearing the wind and rain, I pass the Clear and Bright Festival)   by Wu Wenying ·· 219
48. "Lovely Eyebrows" (Gradually the new moon hangs over the willow trees)   by Wang Yisun ··· 223
49. "A Twig of Mume Blossoms" (The boundless spring grief awaits the pouring of the wine)   by Jiang Jie ·· 229
50. "High Sun Terrace" (Orioles nest in leaves that are closely joined) by Zhang Yan ··· 233

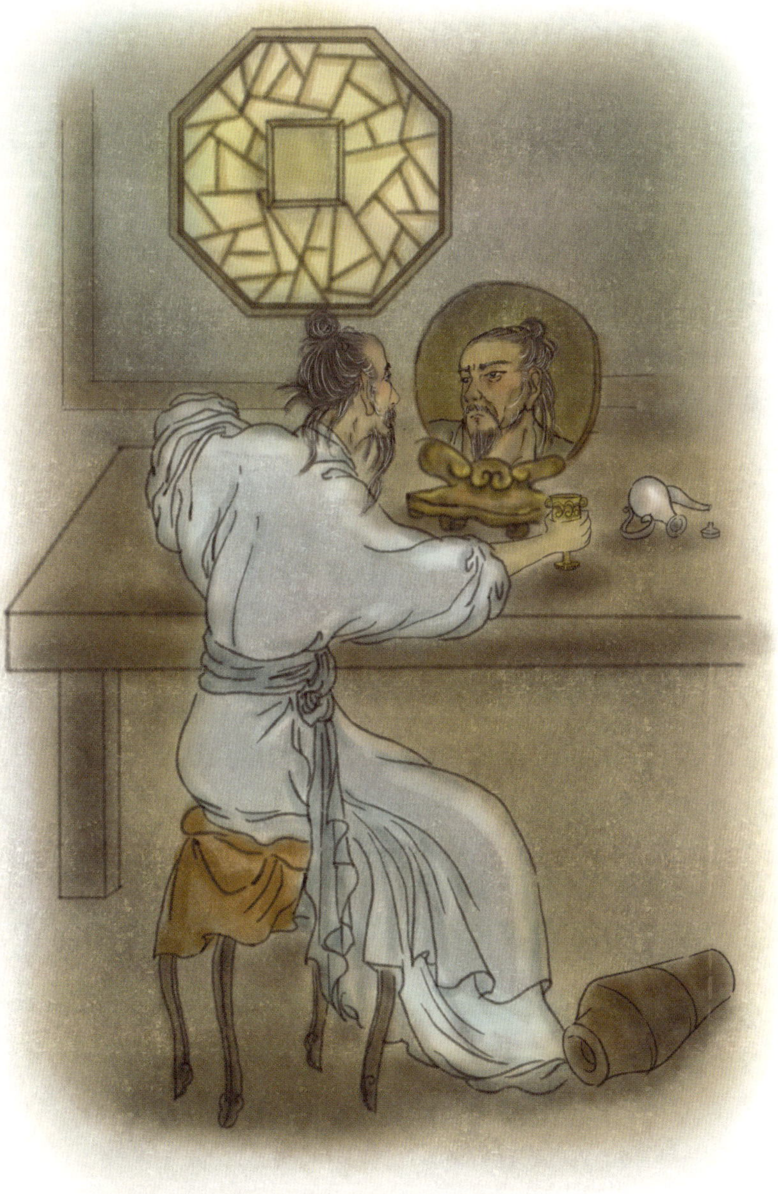

1. 钱惟演《玉楼春·城上风光莺语乱》

【原文】

城上风光莺语乱,城下烟波春拍岸。绿杨芳草几时休?泪眼愁肠先已断。

情怀渐觉成衰晚,鸾镜朱颜惊暗换。昔年多病厌芳尊,今日芳尊惟恐浅。

【释文】

城上风光正好,群莺乱啼;城下春水拍岸,湖面烟波浩渺。这青青杨柳、绵绵芳草何时才会衰败?而我已泪眼蒙眬,愁绪万千,肝肠寸断了。

渐渐觉得自己的情怀已衰朽,同时,还吃惊地发现镜中的容颜也偷偷地发生了变换。往日多病的我总是厌恶去碰那盛着美酒的金杯,如今只恐怕那金杯斟得不够满。

【解析】

这首词是作者的伤春之作。词的上片写景,黄莺啼啭,春水拍岸。而在一片无限的春光里,作者却对着绿杨芳草发出了"几时休"的叹问,情感急转为悲,引出"泪眼愁肠"的悲伤情绪。下片抒情,情怀和容貌都随着时间的推移发生了变化,面对这些,作者唯有借酒浇愁,来抒胸中的烦恼与愁绪。

1. "Jade Tower in Spring" (Chirps of orioles are heard among the glorious scenery in the town) by Qian Weiyan

In the town, chirps of orioles are heard among the glorious scenery. Around of the town, misty waves of springtime are beating against the banks. For how long will the green willows and fragrant grass last? With teary eyes, my melancholic heart is already broken.

My state of mind, as I gradually realized, has become aged. My rosy face in the phoenix patterned mirror, as I surprisingly found, is secretly changing. In the past, I, because of my sickly body, detested the fragrant wine cup. Now I only worry that I am holding a cup which is not fully filled.

【 Commentary 】

This lyric expresses the poet's sad feelings about the passage of spring. The first stanza writes about the scenery: chirps of orioles are heard everywhere and spring water are beating against the banks. In this beautiful season of spring, the poet asks how long the green willows and fragrant grass could last. The question leads to a sudden change of the tone, and "teary eyes and melancholic heart" evoke sad feelings in the readers. The second stanza is featured by lyrical expression. Appearances and sentiments will all change with time, and the poet chooses to drink away the worries and sorrows.

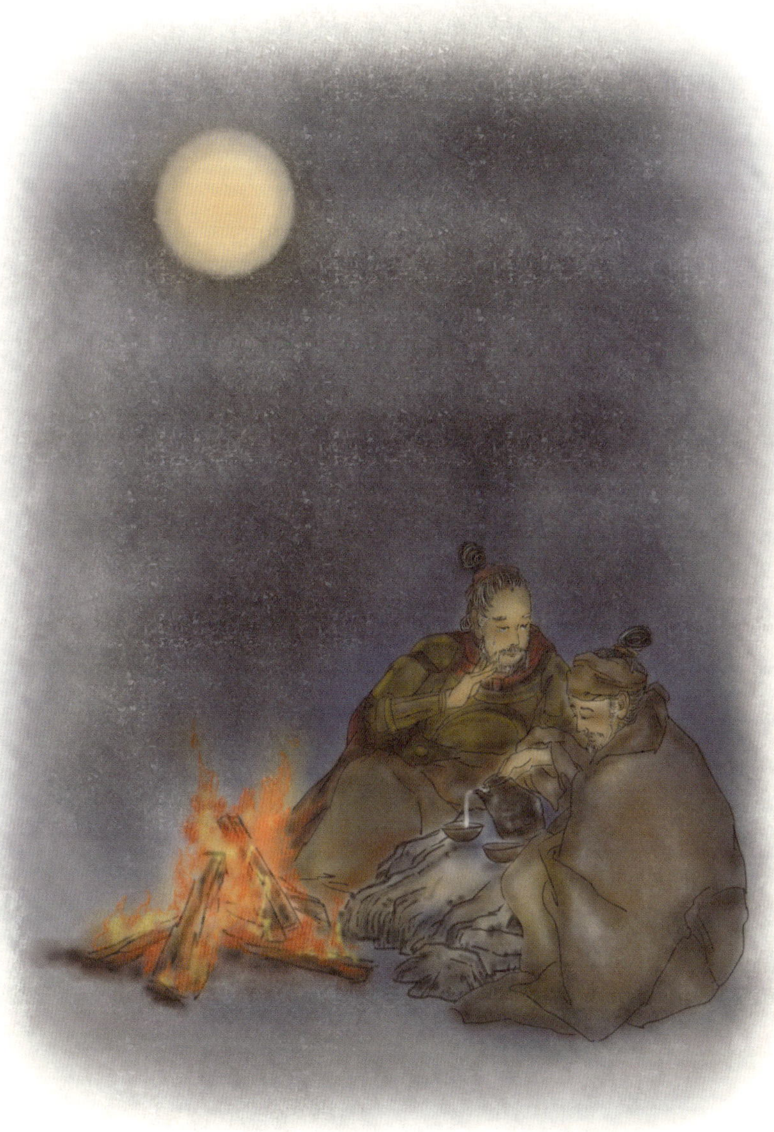

2. 范仲淹《渔家傲·塞下秋来风景异》
秋思

【原文】

塞下秋来风景异,衡阳雁去无留意。四面边声连角起,千嶂里,长烟落日孤城闭。

浊酒一杯家万里,燕然未勒归无计。羌管悠悠霜满地,人不寐,将军白发征夫泪。

【释文】

秋日一到,西北边塞的景色与江南大有不同。大雁也开始向衡阳飞去,毫无留恋之意。随着号角一响,马鸣、风吼等边地的悲鸣之声也随之而起。在层层的山峰环抱中,长烟直上,落日西沉,孤城紧闭。

饮一杯浊酒,思念远在万里之外的家乡。然而边患未除,功业未成,归家之日遥遥无期。在这寒霜洒满大地之时,传来悠悠的羌笛之声。夜渐深,而出征的将军和士兵都无法入睡。随着战事的频仍,他们也愁白了头发,落下无数伤时之泪。

2. "Pride of the Fishermen" (When autumn comes, the scenery becomes different in the border area) by Fan Zhongyan
Thoughts on Autumn

When autumn comes, the scenery becomes different in the border area. Wild geese leave for Hengyang without attention to stay. With the horns, sounds of the frontier rise all round. Among thousands of screen-like peaks, smoke is curling up into the sky; the sun is sinking; the isolated town is shut.

With a rustic wine in hand, I long for my home tens of thousands of miles away. The war is not over and it is impossible to set a return date. Qiang pipe tunes float around and frost covers the ground. People are sleepless; the general's white hair and the soldiers' tears.

【解析】

　　这首词乃词人范仲淹在镇守西北边疆时所作。词的上片写边塞之景,大雁南去、边声四起、长烟落日,一派凄凉壮阔的景象。下片写军中之事,出征的将士一边饮着浊酒,一边思念着家乡,而功业未成的他们有家难回。整首词既表达了词人戍守边疆的决心,也反映了将士们对家乡的思念之情。

【 **Commentary** 】

    This lyric was written by Fan Zhongyan when he was stationed at the border area in northwestern China. The first stanza writes about the desolation and broadness of the frontier scenery: wild geese fly southward; sounds of the frontier rise all around; smoke is curling up into the sky; the sun is setting in the west. The second stanza describes scenes of military camps. Whiling drinking the rustic wine, soldiers long for their hometown, but they cannot return until the war is over. The whole song reveals the resolution of the poet and nostalgia of the soldiers.

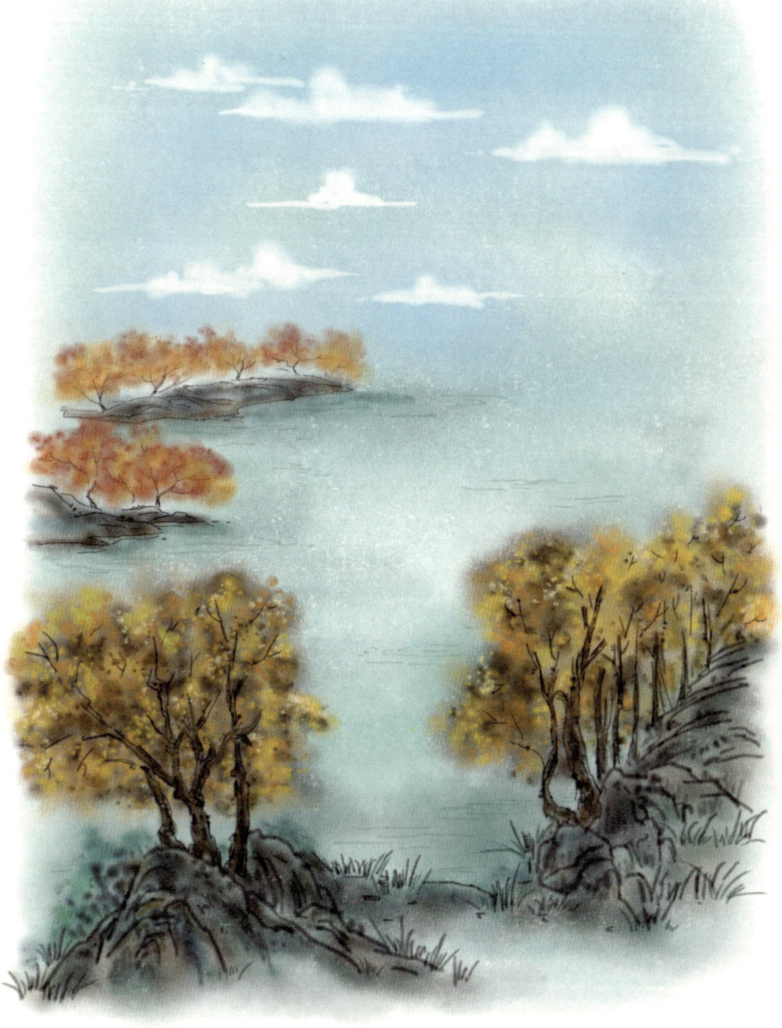

3. 范仲淹《苏幕遮·碧云天》

【原文】

　　碧云天，黄叶地，秋色连波，波上寒烟翠。山映斜阳天接水，芳草无情，更在斜阳外。

　　黯乡魂，追旅思，夜夜除非，好梦留人睡。明月楼高休独倚，酒入愁肠，化作相思泪。

【释文】

　　碧空飘着白云，地上铺满黄叶。秋色绵延至水边，水面泛着清波，一片寒凉而苍翠的雾气笼罩其上。远处的山峦与西下的斜阳相辉映，天与水连成一片。而这无情的芳草延伸至天涯，似乎比斜阳更遥远。

　　因思念家乡而黯然伤神的我，始终抛不开羁旅的愁思。除非夜里做个好梦，才能得以入睡。而此时的明月正映照在高楼之上，还是不要独自倚栏。愁肠百转的我端起酒杯，谁知饮尽之后，都变成了相思的眼泪。

3. "Screened by Southern Curtain" (The sky is blue with clouds) by Fan Zhongyan

The sky is blue with clouds. The ground is covered by yellow leaves. The color of autumn spreads to the waves. Over the waves, cold mist is verdant. The hills glow in the slanting sun; the sky joints the waters. The fragrant grass has no sympathy and grows beyond the slanting sun.

A gloomy homesick soul is obsessed with travel cares. Night after night, unless a pleasant dream can retain me in sleep. In bright moonlight, do not lean alone on rails of the high tower. Wine in sad bowels turns into tears of longing.

【解析】

　　这首词乃去国怀乡之作。词的上片从秋色着笔,进而引出家乡的路远山遥——芳草尽头的故乡,似乎比斜阳还远。下片因景生情,揭示因远离故乡而生发的羁旅之愁。词人只能在梦回故园时才得以安睡,而梦醒之后的月明之夜,却又只能以酒浇愁,徒增伤悲。全词写景时婉转,写情时凄怆,是难得的佳作。

【 Commentary 】

    This lyric was written by a poet who left his country and missed his hometown. The first half starts from the description of autumn color. It then describes the poet's hometown separated by the long distance. His home lies at the end of the grassland, but it seems to be beyond the slanting sun. The second half focuses on the grief evoked by the parting from home. The poet could only rest well when he dreams of his returning to his home. When the dream is startled, he can do nothing but drink away the sorrows, yet this further increases his sorrows. The tone is graceful in scenery depiction and miserable in lyrical expression. The song is indeed an excellent piece.

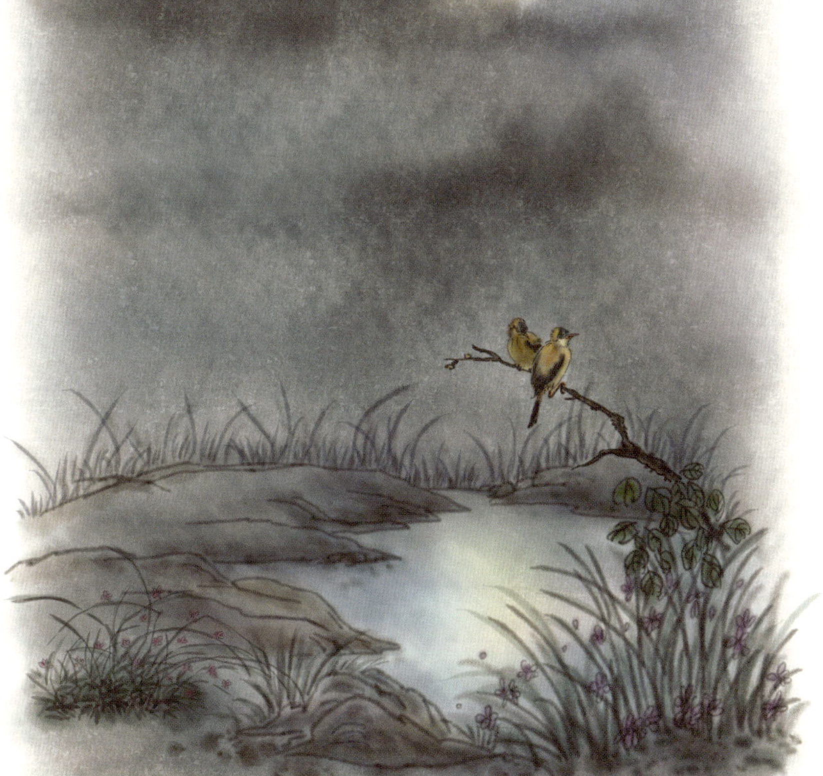

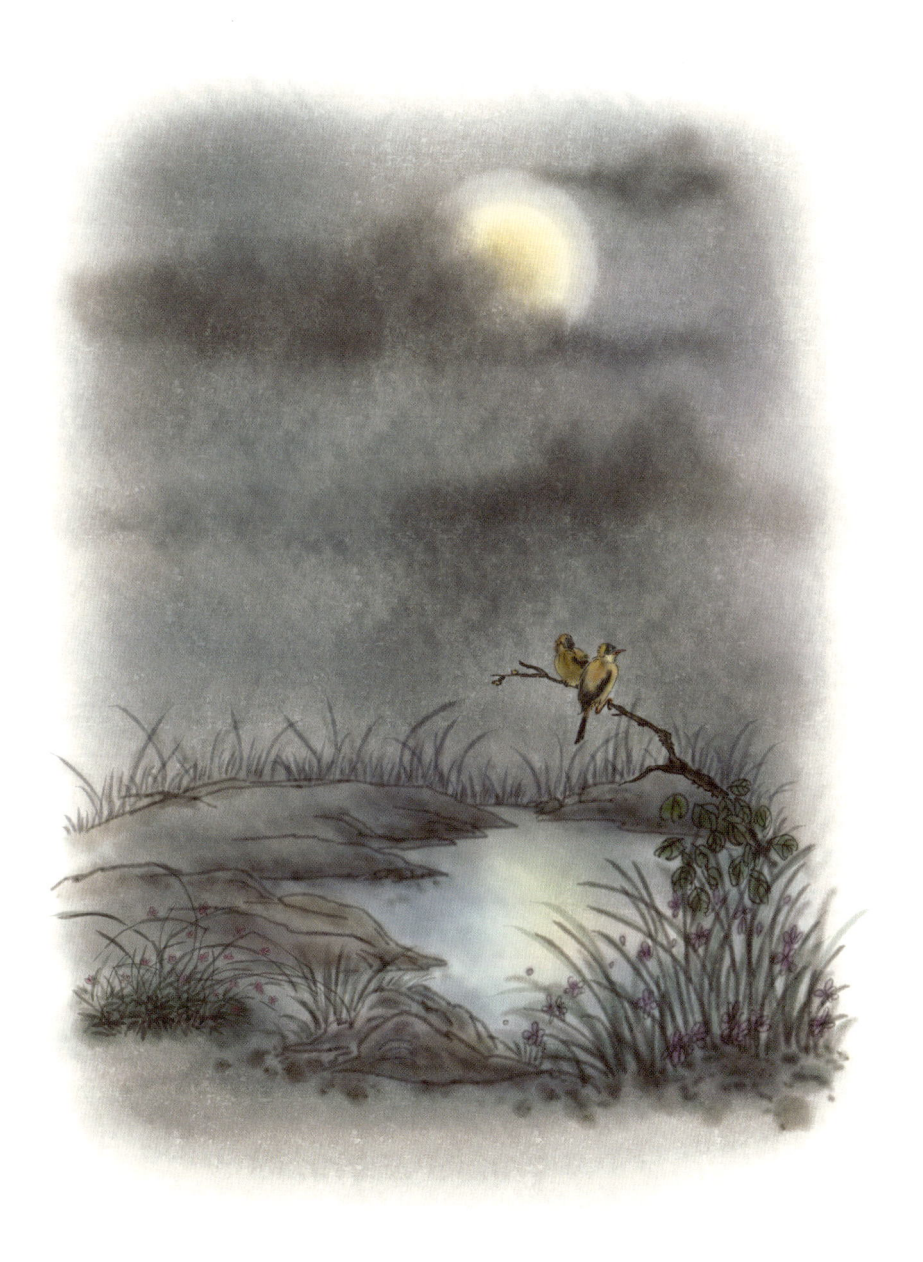

4. 张先《天仙子·水调数声持酒听》

【原文】

时为嘉禾小倅,以病眠,不赴府会。

《水调》数声持酒听,午醉醒来愁未醒。送春春去几时回?临晚镜,伤流景。往事后期空记省。

沙上并禽池上暝,云破月来花弄影。重重帘幕密遮灯,风不定,人初静。明日落红应满径。

【释文】

我一边持杯饮酒,一边听着《水调》的曲子。午间醉酒后人已经醒来,然而心中的愁绪还没有醒。送走了春天,不知道春天什么时候能再回来?傍晚时分,对镜自照,不由得感伤年华似水。那往日的事情和日后的相约,虽然清楚地记得,却也只是徒然。

沙滩上、池塘边成双成对的鸟儿已经歇息。天色渐暗,月亮破云而出,清辉笼罩下的花朵正在摆弄身影。室内重重帘幕低垂,密密地遮住了灯光。而外面的风依旧在吹,人也慢慢安静下来。明日起来,落花应该会铺满小路了。

4. "Heavenly Fairy" (With a wine cup in hand, I listen to the tune of Water Melody)
by Zhang Xian

With a wine cup in hand, I listen to the tune of Water Melody. Awake from afternoon's tipsiness, I have not recovered from grief. I sent spring away and spring is gone, but when will it come back? I look into the mirror at dusk and grieve over the scenes fleeting by. It is no use remembering the past experiences and future appointments.

On the sand stand a pair of waterfowl close to the darkened pond. Clouds break, the moon appears, and flowers play with their own shadows. Layers of curtains closely veil the lamps. Wind is still blowing; others begin to quiet down; tomorrow the fallen redness shall cover the paths all around.

【解析】

　　这首词通过对暮春景致的描写，体现了词人伤春惜春的情怀。开篇以"愁"字点题，词人因伤春和自伤而不自觉地流露出内心的怅惘。下片则以动态来写景，以细微处的表达来反映词人的情绪。尤其一"弄"字，以拟人化的表达生动地写出了月下花朵摇曳的姿态，"着一'弄'字而境界全出矣"（王国维语）。

【 Commentary 】

The scenery description of late spring in this song conveys the sad feelings of the poet who sighs for the passage of time. The first stanza focuses on "grief ", and the sad thoughts on both the season and the poet himself reveal the poet's inner sorrows. The second stanza depicts a scene of dynamic beauty, and the poet's word choice accurately expresses his emotion. For instance, "play with" vividly displays the way flowers sway back and forth underneath the moon. As Wang Guowei (1877-1927) pointed out, "the employment of the word 'play' fully conveyed what the poet felt in real situation".

南詞新譜

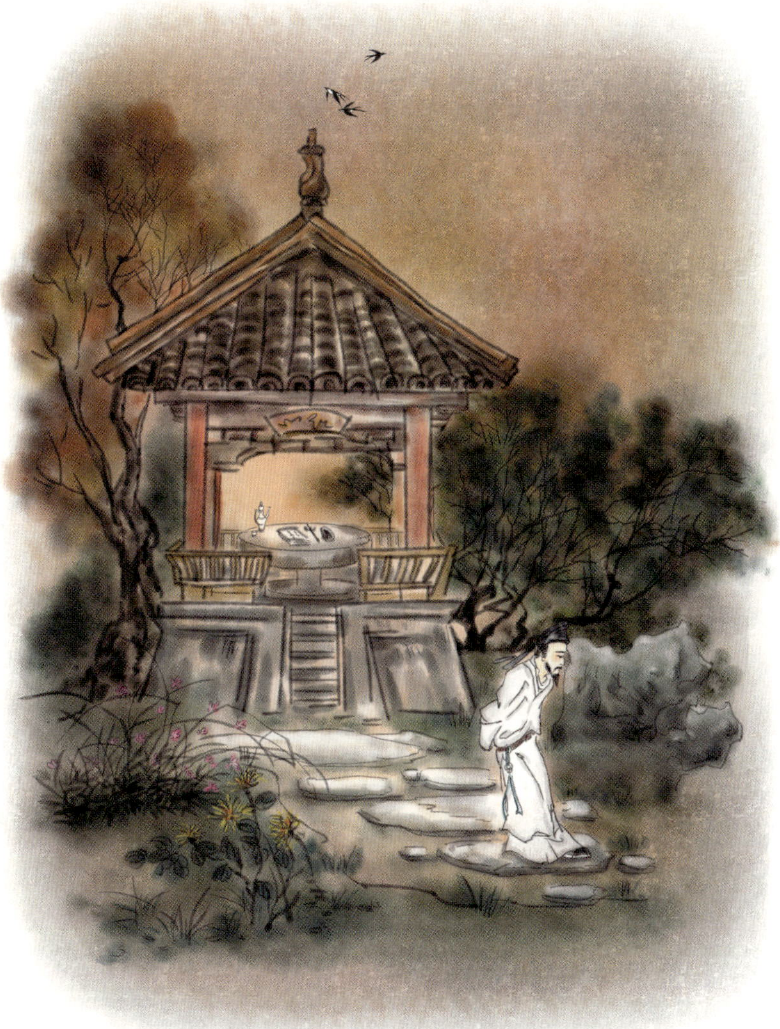

5. 晏殊《浣溪沙·一曲新词酒一杯》

【原文】

　　一曲新词酒一杯,去年天气旧亭台,夕阳西下几时回?
　　无可奈何花落去,似曾相识燕归来。小园香径独徘徊。

【释文】

　　饮一杯美酒、听一曲新词,去年的天气也正是如此,也是在这座亭台上,往事历历在目。而这美好的时光正如西下的夕阳,不知何时才会回来。

　　花儿总要落去,这是令人无可奈何的事。而翩翩归来的燕子又似乎是曾经认识的。如今,这飘满花香的小路,却只剩下我独自徘徊了。

【解析】

　　这首词乃词人伤时感怀之作。回忆往昔,天气、亭台与今日都无差别,但再无美酒可饮、新曲可听,远去的人儿也与新归的燕子不同,失去了消息。词人在抒发别情的同时,也流露出对时光易逝的感叹。"无可奈何花落去,似曾相识燕归来"一联对仗工整,诗意蕴藉,是传诵千古的名句。

5. "Sand at Silk Washing Stream" (A song filled with new words and a cup of wine)
by Yan Shu

A song filled with new words and a cup of wine; in last year's weather and in the old pavilion. The sun is setting in the west, but when will it come back?

Nothing can be done about the flowers that have fallen and gone; swallows that I seem to know come back. I roam alone on the fragrant path of a small garden.

【 Commentary 】

This lyric song was composed by the poet when his sentimentality was evoked by the passage of time. Compared with the experience in the past, the weather and the pavilion are of no difference. But there are no more fine wine or new songs, and those who left him are not as acquainted as the newly returned swallows. While expressing his sorrows on separation, the poet sighs for the fact that time flies past so easily. The first couplet of the second stanza is rich in meaning and popular for hundreds of years.

南雅詞鈔

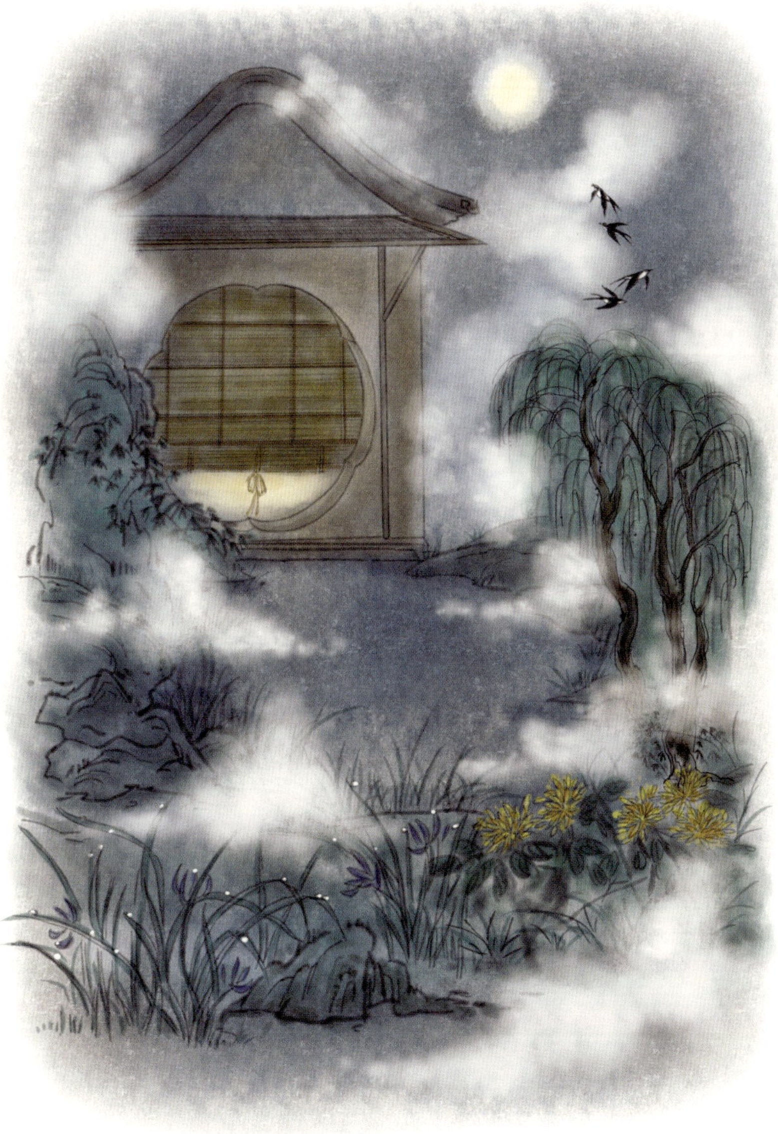

6. 晏殊《蝶恋花·槛菊愁烟兰泣露》

【原文】

槛菊愁烟兰泣露,罗幕轻寒,燕子双飞去。明月不谙离恨苦,斜光到晓穿朱户。

昨夜西风凋碧树,独上高楼,望尽天涯路。欲寄彩笺兼尺素,山长水阔知何处?

【释文】

花池里的菊花被烟雾笼罩,似乎正在忧愁,兰草挂着露珠,也像是在哭泣。丝罗做的帘幕之间透着些许寒意,燕子双双飞去。明月不懂得离别之苦,皎洁的月光斜照在屋内直到破晓。

昨夜西风骤至,绿树上枝叶凋零。我独自登上这高高的城楼,望着那绵绵的道路消失在天涯的尽头。想要寄一封信给远方的人儿,可是山水阻隔,道路遥远,我思念的人究竟在何处?

【解析】

此词虽为伤秋怀人之作,但意境高远。上片描写苑中景物,"愁烟""泣露"将菊花、兰花这些景物拟人化,将词人的主观情感寓于其中,点出离恨的主题;下片承离恨而来,视野由内而外,词人登楼远望,而绿树凋零,与心上人儿又山水阻隔,故愁思渐浓。

6. "Butterflies Linger with Flowers" (Beside the balustrade, chrysanthemums are sad in mist and orchids are shedding tears of dew) by Yan Shu

Beside the balustrade, chrysanthemums are sad in mist and orchids are shedding tears of dew. Silk curtains are swaying in light chill. A pair of swallows side by side flies away. The bright moon does not know the grief and bitterness of parting. Its slanting rays are piercing the vermilion doors till dawn breaks.

Last night the western wind faded the green trees. I ascended to the high tower to take a view toward the end of the road. I wanted to send my love notes and letters. But the mountains are high; the rivers are wide; I do not know where you are.

【 Commentary 】

In this lyric, the poet sighs for the arrival of autumn and longs for the beloved person far away. But readers could feel a sense of loftiness and positiveness. The first half outlines a garden scene. The poet personified the chrysanthemums and orchids by employing the words such as "sad" and "shedding tears". In so doing, he entrusted his own feelings and emotions to the description and highlighted the theme of parting grief. The poet changed his point of view in the second stanza from the internals to the externals. He climbed up the high tower to look into the distance. The falling leaves of the green trees as well as his beloved one who was separated by mountains and rivers further increased his sorrows.

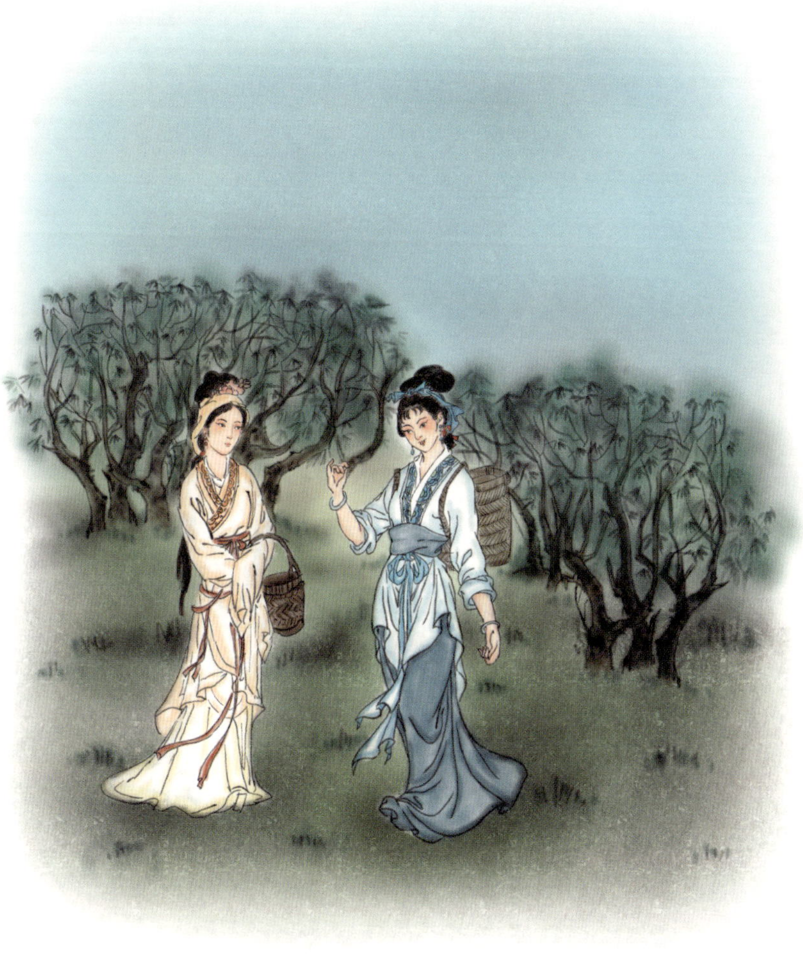

7. 晏殊《破阵子·燕子来时新社》

【原文】

燕子来时新社,梨花落后清明。池上碧苔三四点,叶底黄鹂一两声,日长飞絮轻。

巧笑东邻女伴,采桑径里逢迎。疑怪昨宵春梦好,元是今朝斗草赢,笑从双脸生。

【释文】

春社之时,梨花渐衰而清明将至,燕子从南方飞来。几点碧绿的水苔点缀着池面,不时从树叶间传来几声黄鹂的叫声,柳絮纷飞,白昼正在渐渐转长。

采桑的小路上遇着笑脸盈盈的东邻女伴。难道是昨晚做了一个春宵好梦(才让她如此愉快)?非也,原来是因为今天斗草胜利啊,笑容不由得从她的双颊浮现出来。

【解析】

该篇乃写春末夏初的景致。上片写景,笔调清新;下片侧面描写采桑少女斗草嬉戏,简单的笔墨间人物的神态、心理等便被刻画得十分细致。全文极具生活气息。

7. "Breaking the Formation" (When the swallows return, it is the New Communal Day) by Yan Shu

When the swallows return, it is the New Communal Day. After pear blossoms fall, it is the Clear and Bright Day. On the pond, there are two or three patches of verdant moss. Under the leaves, one or two snatches of oriole chirps. The day is long, and the flying willow catkins are light.

A pretty smile was on my female friend's face from eastern neighborhood, and I met her on the path among mulberry trees. I wonder whether it was because last night her spring dream was good. It turned out to be the victory in today's grass-cutting game. A smile was emerging and spreading across two cheeks.

【Commentary】

This lyric depicts the scene of late spring and early summer. The first stanza writes about the scenery and its plain language brings a sense of freshness. The second stanza indirectly describes the grass-cutting game. The simple depiction of facial expression and internal thoughts is extremely impressive. The whole song is full of life.

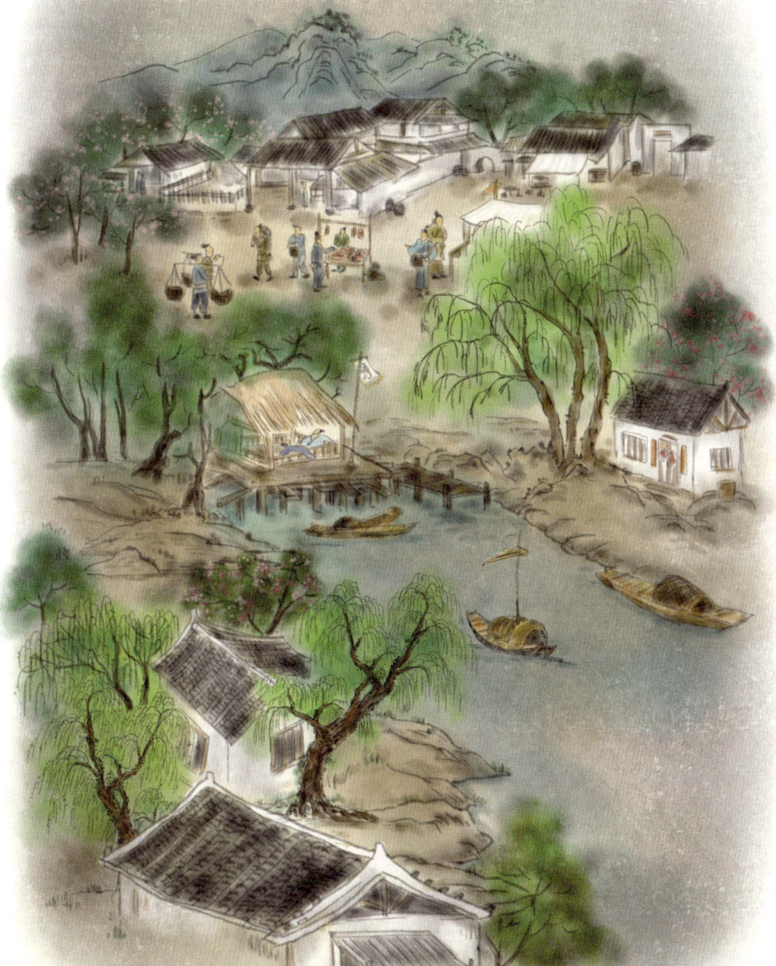

8. 宋祁《玉楼春·东城渐觉风光好》

【原文】

东城渐觉风光好,縠皱波纹迎客棹。绿杨烟外晓寒轻,红杏枝头春意闹。

浮生长恨欢娱少,肯爱千金轻一笑。为君持酒劝斜阳,且向花间留晚照。

【释文】

漫步东城,渐渐觉得此地的风光越来越好,水波荡漾,似乎在迎接往来的客船。拂晓时分,如烟的杨柳笼罩在些许的寒意之中;而开满红杏的枝头上,已是春意盎然。

常常遗憾人生无常,欢乐太少,怎么还会吝惜钱财而轻视快乐的生活?那就让我为你举起杯中之酒奉劝夕阳,请将余晖在花丛中多留些时间吧。

【解析】

这首词上片写春景之美,揭示了"风光好"的主题;下片感叹人生飘忽不定,"浮生若梦",不如潇洒度日。全篇很少修饰和雕琢,但描写极为生动,尤其"红杏枝头春意闹"一句,因为对"闹"字的不同理解,历来赢得了很多赞誉,也引起了一些讨论。

8. "Spring in Jade Tower" (The scenery in the eastern city seems gradually to be fine) by Song Qi

The scenery in the eastern city seems gradually to be fine. The silken ripples greet the oars of the passenger boats. Beyond the misty green willows, morning chill is light. Over the twigs of apricot flowers the spirit of spring glows.

In this floating life, I always regret having little pleasure and entertainment. How could I value a thousand pieces of gold over a smile? For you, I hold my wine cup and persuade the slanting sun, to stay and leave among flowers its evening glow.

【 Commentary 】

The first stanza describes the beauty of the spring season, and reveals the theme of "fine scenery." In the second stanza, the poet sighs for the uncertain nature of human life. Since "the floating life is like a dream," it is better to spend one's time at one's ease. There are very few embellishments or fancy words, but the description is fairly vivid. In the line "over the twigs of apricot flowers the spirit of spring glows," different opinions arise concerning the word "glows." Readers who appreciated the word were many, but there were others who thought it might need to be further considered.

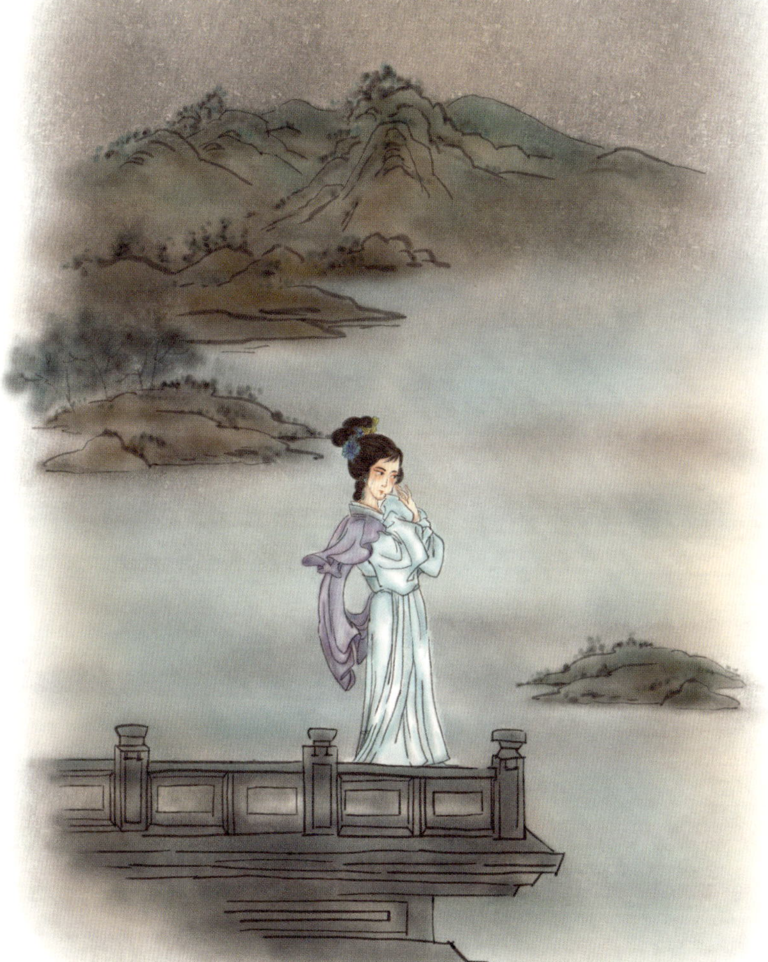

9. 欧阳修《踏莎行·候馆梅残》

【原文】

　　候馆梅残,溪桥柳细,草薰风暖摇征辔。离愁渐远渐无穷,迢迢不断如春水。

　　寸寸柔肠,盈盈粉泪,楼高莫近危栏倚。平芜尽处是春山,行人更在春山外。

【释文】

　　客舍中的梅花已经残败落去,溪桥边新生的细柳低垂,在风暖草香中,离别的人儿正骑马远行。随着脚步越远,离愁也变得无穷无尽,正如这绵绵不断流向远方的春水。

　　留在家中的人肝肠寸断,眼泪和着脂粉流淌。还是不要登上高楼倚着栏杆远望,这旷野的尽头是春山,而思念的远行之人还在春山之外啊。

【解析】

　　这首词写离情。上片从行人的角度着笔,写随着行程越远,春色越浓,离别之情越强烈;下片以闺中人的视角,写其登高望远,思念之愁连绵不绝。全篇语言浅白而意义深远,"不厌百回读"。

9. "Treading on Grass" (Around the inn, the plums are withered) by Ouyang Xiu

Around the inn, the plums are withered; by the stream bridge, the willows look thin. The fragrance of grass in warm breezes; I sway the reins. The further I march, the more my parting grief grows, and it is growing nonstop, just like spring water spreading far, far away.

Inches of broken heart and lines of rouge-mixed tears; do not approach and lean on the balustrades of tall buildings. At the end of the flat grassland lie the spring mountains. The traveler is beyond those spring mountains.

【 Commentary 】

This lyric focuses on separation. The first stanza was written from the perspective of the traveler. The further the traveler moves on, the more intense the spring color becomes and the parting sorrow grows. The second stanza was written from a chamber lady's angle. She ascends the high buildings and looks into the distance, but her grief and longing for her beloved seems endless. The language in this song is plain but meaningful, and "one will not feel bored even after reading it for a hundred times".

南詞敘錄

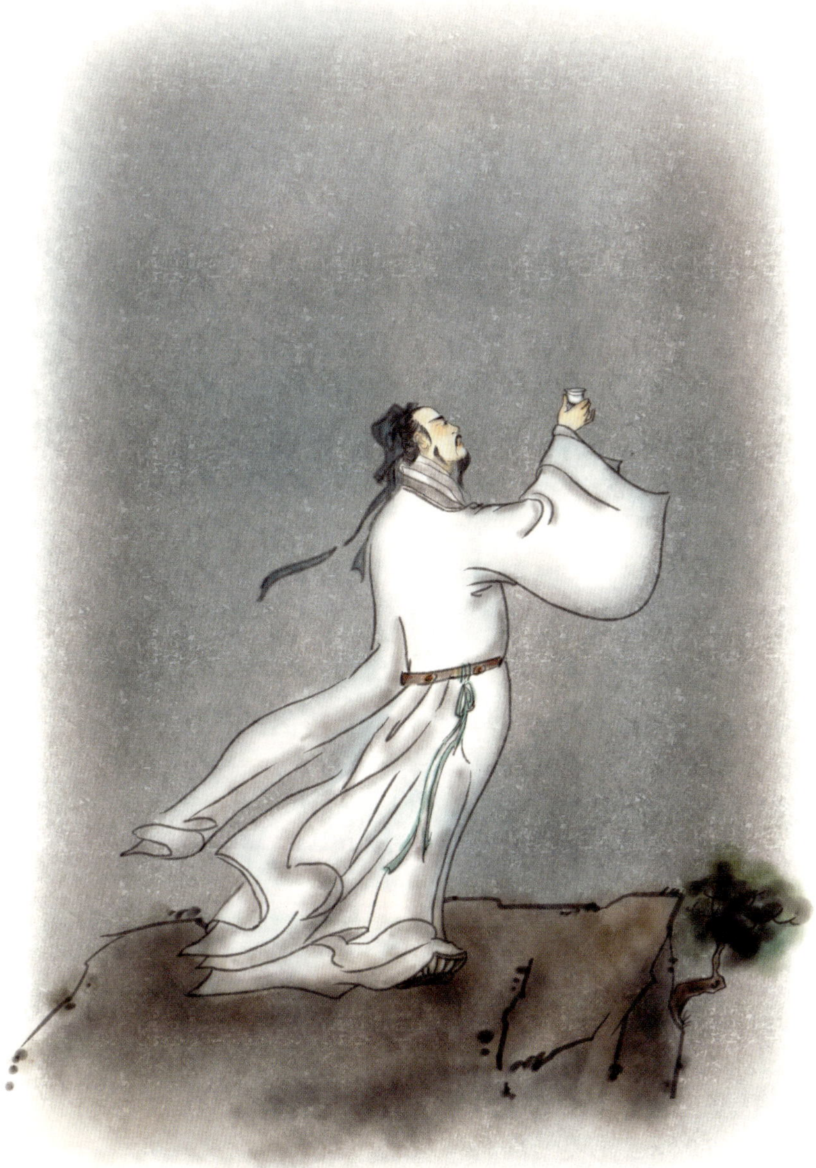

10. 欧阳修《浪淘沙·把酒祝东风》

【原文】

把酒祝东风,且共从容。垂杨紫陌洛城东,总是当时携手处,游遍芳丛。

聚散苦匆匆,此恨无穷。今年花胜去年红,可惜明年花更好,知与谁同?

【释文】

我举起酒杯向东风祝告,请它在此多停留些时光。想起洛阳城东垂着杨柳的小路,我们当年曾在那里携手同游,片片花丛都曾留下我们的足迹。

相聚和别离都是这样匆忙,只留下无限的遗憾。今年的花开得比去年的更加红艳,明年的花会开得更好,可惜到那时不知道还能与谁一起游赏?

【解析】

这首词乃词人与友人重游洛阳城东旧地时,怀念往日的相聚时光,有感而作。词的上片由眼前之境而忆往日之境,下片则由当下之境而设想未来之境。对于友谊的珍惜,对于时光易逝、聚散匆匆的感慨蕴含其中。

10. "Waves Dredging Sand" (Holding a wine cup, I drink a toast to eastern wind)
by Ouyang Xiu

Holding a wine cup, I drink a toast to eastern wind; why don't you linger in my company? Under drooping willows and on violet pathways east of Luoyang, we used to hold hands in bygone days, strolling past all flower shrubs.

Gathering and then scattering, always bitterly in haste, leaves forever regrets. This year's flowers are redder than last year's, and next year's may be even redder, but who knows whom I will enjoy them with?

【 Commentary 】

The poet revisited the eastern part of Luoyang city with his friend and recalled their happy reunions in the past. It was this experience that inspired him to write the song lyric. While standing in a place where he visited before, the poet recollects the bygones days in the first stanza and anticipates the future in the second. The cherishment of friendship, lamentation over passage of time, and the sigh for the reunion in haste are all embodied in this song.

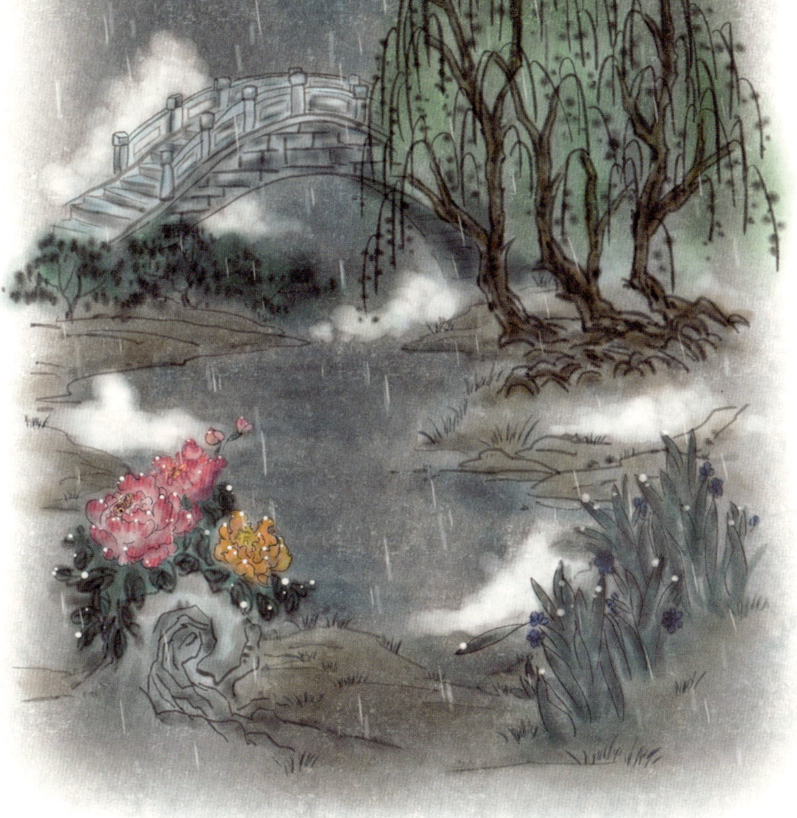

11. 欧阳修《蝶恋花·庭院深深深几许》

【原文】

庭院深深深几许,杨柳堆烟,帘幕无重数。玉勒雕鞍游冶处,楼高不见章台路。

雨横风狂三月暮,门掩黄昏,无计留春住。泪眼问花花不语,乱红飞过秋千去。

【释文】

庭院是如此深邃,它到底有多深呢?杨柳依依,聚起阵阵烟雾,像是形成层层苍翠的帘幕。豪门大户的车马停满了游乐的地方,即使站在高楼之上,我也望不见这寻欢作乐的处所。

狂风暴雨中,三月即将过去。黄昏中我掩上门,遗憾没有办法将春天留住。泪眼蒙眬中去问花儿,花儿也不应答。只在一阵风后,零落地飞到秋千那边去了。

【解析】

此词上片写王孙公子耽于游乐,首句连用三个"深"字,既写出了庭院之深,也暗示闺阁之深,闺中女子与外界隔绝之深。下片通过暮春时节恶劣的天气,来象征闺中女子的境遇——青春年华同花一样败落,无法留住。整首词情景交融,受到历来评论家的称赏。

11. "Butterflies Linger over Flowers" (So deep is the courtyard, but how deep is it)
by Ouyang Xiu

So deep is the courtyard, but how deep is it? Willows heap on heap are like smoke, forming endless layers of screens and curtains. A jade bridle, a sculpted saddle and the pleasure-seeking arena; the tower is high and the road of Terrace of Seal cannot be seen.

The rain and wind are raging at the late period of the third month. I close the door in the dusk, but there is no way to hold spring. With my teary eyes, I ask the flowers, but the flowers are wordless. A chaos of redness flies across swings.

【 Commentary 】

The first stanza indicates that sons of the royal families and nobilities indulge themselves in pleasure. The poet uses the character "deep" for three times in the first line, and this reveals the courtyard is indeed deep and the lady in the chamber is isolated from the outside world. In the second stanza, the unfavorable weather in late spring is likened to the situation of the lady in the chamber: for the prime time is gone and there is no way to keep it. Scenery depiction and lyrical expression harmoniously blend in this song and it has been regarded as an excellent piece by critics in later generations.

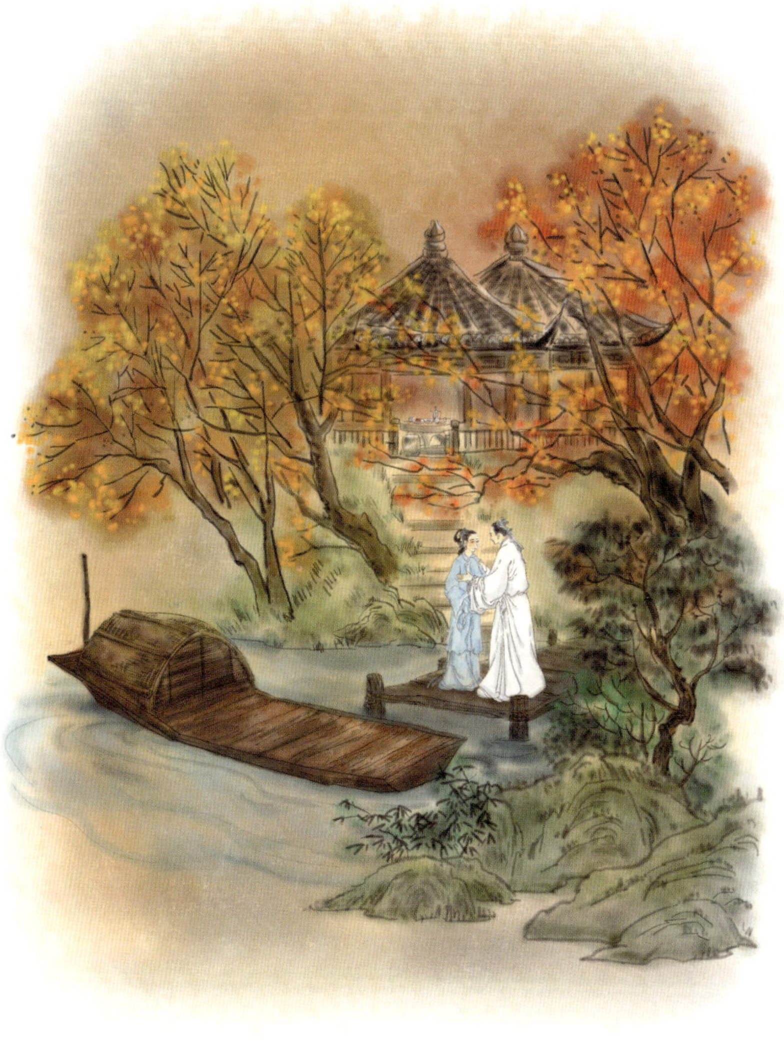

12. 柳永《雨霖铃·寒蝉凄切》

【原文】

　　寒蝉凄切，对长亭晚，骤雨初歇。都门帐饮无绪，留恋处，兰舟催发。执手相看泪眼，竟无语凝噎。念去去，千里烟波，暮霭沉沉楚天阔。

　　多情自古伤离别，更那堪冷落清秋节！今宵酒醒何处？杨柳岸，晓风残月。此去经年，应是良辰好景虚设。便纵有千种风情，更与何人说？

【释文】

　　初秋时分，寒蝉悲鸣，有凄凉之感。面对长亭，不觉天色渐晚，一场急骤的雨刚刚才停下来。在这京城的郊外，设帐宴饮送行，然而毫无欢乐的情绪。正在留恋不舍时，快要出发的船儿已来催促。我们泪眼蒙眬，紧握彼此的手，然而喉咙竟像是被塞住了，一句话也说不出来。想着将要不断远去，望着这一望无际烟雾弥漫的水面，云雾缭绕，天色昏沉，楚地的天空显得多么寥廓啊！

　　多情的人自古以来容易为离别而感伤，更何况是在这样冷落的清秋时节。今夜酒醒，我又将身在何处？怕是在那杨柳岸边，只有拂晓的凉风和残破的月儿相伴。此次离开，年复一年，美好的时光、宜人的景色，都将形同虚设。纵然有千百种情意，又向谁去诉说呢？

12. "Bells Ringing in the Rain" (Cold cicadas are chirping dolefully) by Liu Yong

Cold cicadas are chirping dolefully. We face the long pavilion at dusk and a sudden rain has just stopped. In the tent at capital gate, we are in no mood for a farewell toast. While we are lingering for a while, the orchid boat impels me to depart. Holding hands and looking into each other's tearful eyes, we both choked, unable to utter a word. I think of my voyage through thousands of miles of misty waves. The evening mist is heavy and the sky of Chu kingdom is vast.

Lovers have, since ancient times, suffered from the grief of parting, and how could we bear it in such a cold and clear autumn day! Where would I wake up from my drink tonight? At a willowy bank with a dawning breeze and a waning moon. This parting will last for years, and good times and fine sceneries would appear in vain. Even though I have a thousand varieties of delicate feelings, with whom can I share them?

【解析】

　　这首词乃柳永作品中最负盛名之作。上片先写离别的环境，开头十二字，点明时间、地点及送别的氛围。紧接着具体写送别的情景，船工急催，而泪眼相对，竟说不出话来，只能望向一望无际的水面和天空。下片主要抒情，通过想象叙写别离后的光景：分别之后，即使风光再好，但没有心爱的人可以诉说，一切也就失去了意义。整首词真挚感人，乃叙写离情别绪的佳作。

【 Commentary 】

This is the most famous lyric written by Liu Yong. The first stanza starts with the description of the parting scene. The first twelve characters tell the readers about the time, the place and the atmosphere. The following lines are detailed descriptions: the boatman impelled the poet to depart; the two lovers looked into each other's teary eyes; they could not utter one word; they looked into the water and sky in distance. The second stanza mainly expresses the poet's emotion. He imagines what would happen after the separation: if his beloved is not around, everything will turn out to be meaningless, albeit with the beautiful scenery. This sincere and moving piece is an exemplar in writing about the parting sorrows.

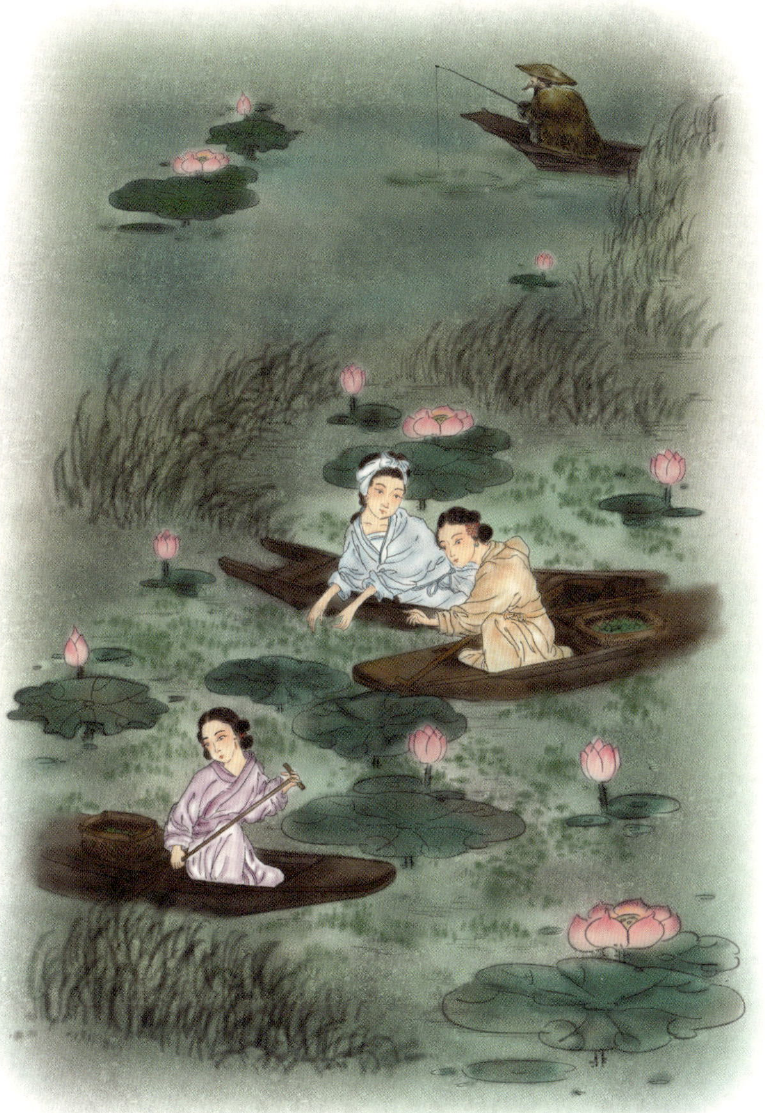

13. 柳永《望海潮·东南形胜》

【原文】

　　东南形胜,三吴都会,钱塘自古繁华。烟柳画桥,风帘翠幕,参差十万人家。云树绕堤沙,怒涛卷霜雪,天堑无涯。市列珠玑,户盈罗绮,竞豪奢。

　　重湖叠巘清嘉。有三秋桂子,十里荷花。羌管弄晴,菱歌泛夜,嬉嬉钓叟莲娃。千骑拥高牙,乘醉听箫鼓,吟赏烟霞。异日图将好景,归去凤池夸。

【释文】

　　杭州乃地理形势优越的地方,为吴兴、吴郡、会稽三吴之地,人口集中的城市。这里自古就十分繁华富庶。放眼城中,到处是如烟笼罩的柳树和装饰华美的桥梁。挡风的帘子和翠绿色的帷幕掩映下,房屋高低参差,住着十万户左右的人家。高耸入云的大树环绕着沙堤,汹涌的波涛卷起霜雪似的白色浪花,钱塘江江面广阔无边。市场上陈列着各种珍贵的物品,家家户户充满了绫罗绸缎,大家争着表现自己的奢华。

　　西湖的内外湖及四周重叠的山峦,风景都清秀美丽。九月的桂花飘香,十里荷花正艳。晴朗的日子,处处都在演奏着音乐;夜晚

13. "Seeing Sea Tide" (Located in the southeast)
by Liu Yong

Located in the southeast, and joining the Three Wu regions, Qiantang since ancient times has been prosperous. Misty willows and patterned bridges; windproof curtains and green screens; ten myriads of houses, high and low. Cloudy trees circle around bank sands; enraged billows roll up frost and snow; celestial moat is boundless. Markets display pearls and treasure; silk and satin fill households; one is vying with another for prodigality and luxury.

The inner and outer lakes, and the hills tier upon tier, are clear and fine. There are the autumn osmanthus flowers, and lotus flowers across ten miles. Mongol flutes play with the sunny day. Songs from waternut plucking boats float at night. Happy are the old fishermen and lotus plucking maidens. One thousand horsemen accompany the high official. In tipsy, they listen to the vertical flutes and drums, and appreciate and chant the misty rosy clouds. I will outline the beautiful scenery some other day, and praise it when I return the phoenix pond.

时分，采菱船上清歌飞扬。钓鱼的老翁、采莲的姑娘，各个笑逐颜开。浩浩荡荡的骑兵队伍簇拥着长官，趁着醉意听吹箫打鼓之声，观赏、吟唱这美丽的湖光山色。他日将这美好的景致描画出来，回到朝廷之时，好向人们夸耀。

【解析】

　　这首词概括地描写了北宋时期，杭州一带的秀丽景色及繁华富庶的景象。据说金朝皇帝完颜亮听到这首词，对"九月桂花飘香，十里荷花正艳"这样的盛景十分向往，所以起了南征宋朝之心，可见此词的影响力之广。

【 Commentary 】

This lyric outlines a scenic and prosperous picture of Hangzhou city during the Northern Song (960—1127) dynasty. It was said that Wanyan Liang (1122—1161), the emperor of Jin (1115—1234) dynasty, had long been yearning for such a magnificent city since he read this lyric, especially the scenic picture in which "the fragrances of the osmanthus in the ninth month fill the air and the lotus flowers across ten miles are blooming beautifully." Hence, it aroused his desire to conquer the Southern Song (1127—1279) dynasty. This indicates the song has been very well received.

南詞選譯

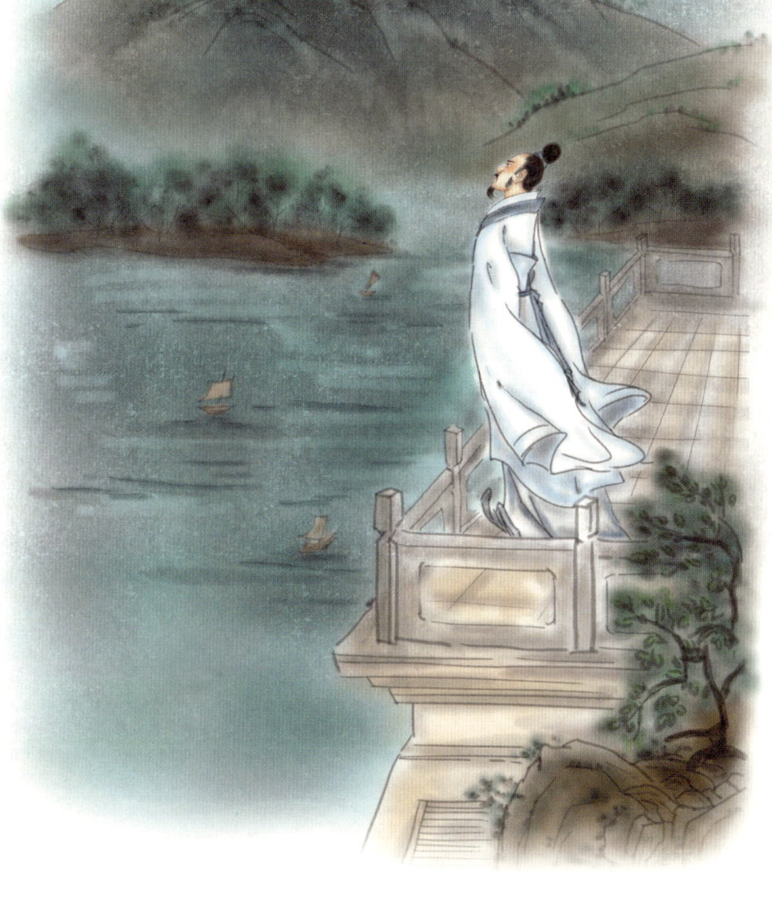

14. 柳永《八声甘州·对潇潇暮雨洒江天》

【原文】

　　对潇潇暮雨洒江天，一番洗清秋。渐霜风凄紧，关河冷落，残照当楼。是处红衰翠减，苒苒物华休。唯有长江水，无语东流。

　　不忍登高临远，望故乡渺邈，归思难收。叹年来踪迹，何事苦淹留？想佳人，妆楼颙望，误几回、天际识归舟。争知我，倚栏杆处，正恁凝愁！

【释文】

　　傍晚时分，一阵潇潇急雨从江边的天际洒落，将这秋日景致洗得更加明澈。寒风裹着秋霜，渐渐凄冷逼人。关塞山河都变得萧条冷落，落日的余晖刚好照射到我所在的高楼之上。一眼望去，处处红花枯萎、绿叶凋零，美好的景物渐渐都已消失。只有长江水，默默地向东流去。

　　不忍心再去登上高楼，凝望远方。看那故乡是如此遥远，我归家的思绪，实在难以抑制。叹息这几年来四处漂泊流浪，到底为什么要久留他乡，迟迟不归呢？遥想在故乡的心上之人，也一定是在高楼之上，痴痴抬头凝望。几次错把从江边天际归去的船儿，认成是我的归船。她又怎知道，我也正在此处倚栏远望，忧愁凝结，无法排解呢！

14. "Ganzhou Melody of Eight Rhymes" (I face the pattering rain in the evening pouring from river sky) by Liu Yong

I face the pattering rain in the evening pouring from river sky. At one sweep, it washes the clear autumn. Gradually the frosty wind becomes bleak and strong; the pass and rivers are chilly and desolate; the afterglow of the setting sun is on the tower. Here, the red fades and the green decreases, and gradually the essences of everything die out. Only the water of the Yangtze River wordlessly flows to the east.

I can hardly bear to climb high and look into the distant. When I gaze at the hometown, it is remote and far. My thoughts on returning home are hard to control. I sigh for years of traces left, and why should I stay out for long? I think of the fine lady; in her boudoir, she must have looked into the distance, and mistaken for many times for my returning boat from the heaven border. How could she have known that I am leaning against the balustrade and suffering from sorrowful thoughts?

【解析】

  这首词描写离人之愁。上片写景,用清秋寥落衰败之景来写思乡之愁;下片抒情,从对方着笔,遥想留在家中的心上人也一定在思念自己,与杜甫《月夜》中"今夜鄜州月,闺中只独看。遥怜小儿女,未解忆长安"有异曲同工之妙。

【 Commentary 】

This lyric writes about a traveler's sorrows. In the first stanza, the desolate scene of the autumn evokes the poet's nostalgia. The poet mentions his beloved in the second stanza. His wife at home must have been thinking about himself. This stanza is similar to the poem "A Moonlight Night" by Du Fu: "The moon is hanging over Fuzhou tonight. My beloved could only watch it in the chamber alone. I miss my little children in my faraway home. They do not understand why their mother longs for Chang'an."

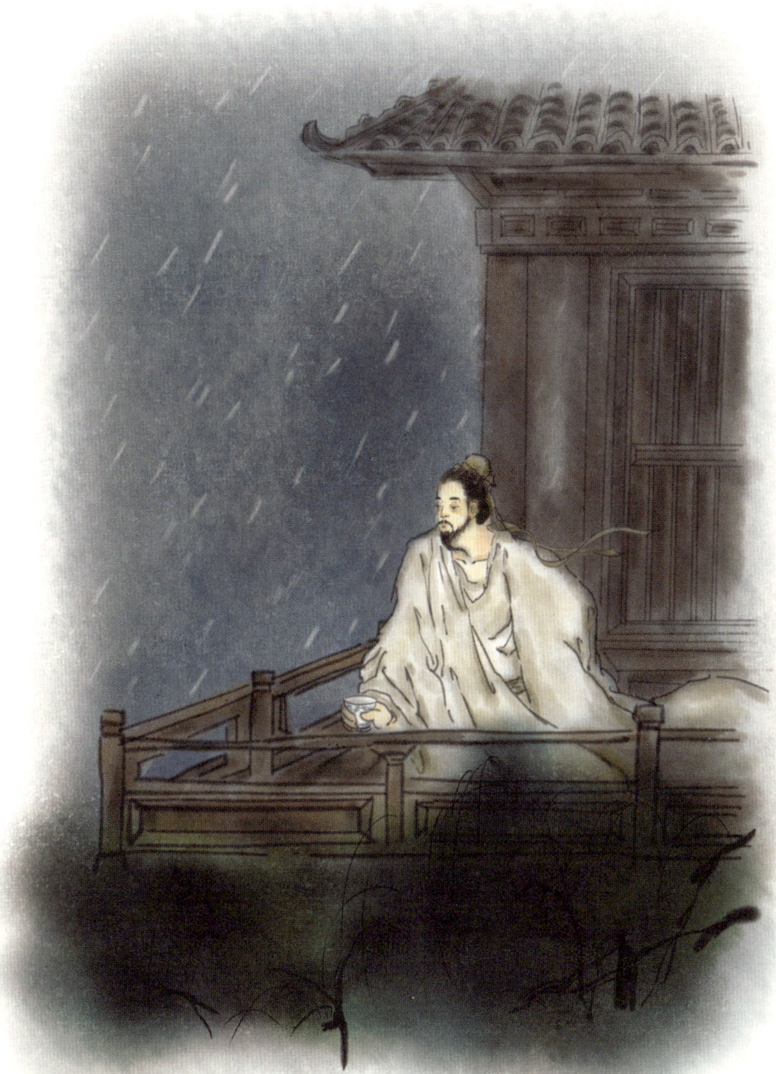

15. 柳永《蝶恋花·伫倚危楼风细细》

【原文】

伫倚危楼风细细,望极春愁,黯黯生天际。草色烟光残照里,无言谁会凭栏意?

拟把疏狂图一醉。对酒当歌,强乐还无味。衣带渐宽终不悔,为伊消得人憔悴。

【释文】

在高楼上久久站立,细细的微风拂面。向远处眺望,春日的愁思仿佛凄然地从天边升起来。碧绿的草色、烟雾的光晕,都笼罩在残阳的余晖中。而我默默凭栏远眺的心意,谁能理解呢?

打算不受礼法的拘束来博得一醉,然而饮酒听曲,勉强作乐,终究还是索然无味。而我也因此渐渐消瘦,衣带宽松,但我始终不会后悔,宁愿为了她而相思憔悴。

【解析】

这是一首相思怀人之作。词的上片以写景为主,词人倚楼远望,草色、烟光、残阳,都反衬出词人的春日之愁。下片点明愁思之因,原来是为思念之人而憔悴消瘦。但结尾处词人表明,即使为她消瘦憔悴,也终不后悔,使全词的感情得到了升华。

15. "Butterflies Linger with Flowers" (In light and soft breeze, I lean against the balustrade on a high tower) by Liu Yong

In light and soft breeze, I lean against the balustrade on a high tower; as I gaze into the distance, spring sorrow dolefully rises from the skyline. The color of grass and the haze of smoke are in the glow of sunset. Without words, who would understand why I am leaning against the balustrade?

I tend to indulge myself in drinking. Facing the wine, I would sing, but strained mirth brings no good mood. My clothes are getting loose gradually, but I will never regret; it is worthwhile growing languid for my love.

【 Commentary 】

This lyric mainly writes about lovesickness. The first half focuses on scenery description. Leaning on the railings on a high tower, the poet looks into the distance. The color of the grass, the haze of the smoke, and the setting sun all highlight the poet's grief on a spring day. The second half offers the reason for the grief: the longing for his beloved. In the end, the poet states that he will not feel regretful even if the lovesickness causes him to grow haggard. The last couplet brings the value of the whole lyric to a higher level.

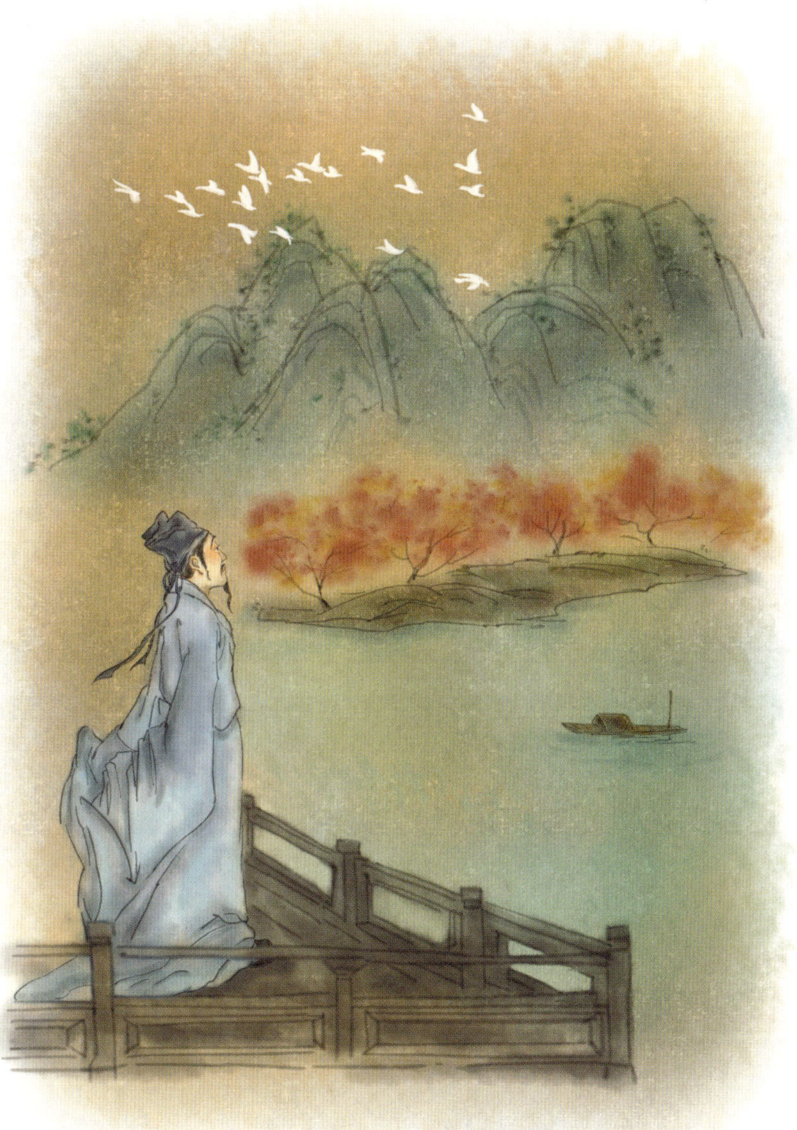

16. 王安石《桂枝香·登临送目》

【原文】

　　登临送目，正故国晚秋，天气初肃。千里澄江似练，翠峰如簇。征帆去棹残阳里，背西风，酒旗斜矗。彩舟云淡，星河鹭起，画图难足。

　　念往昔，豪华竞逐，叹门外楼头，悲恨相续。千古凭高对此，漫嗟荣辱。六朝旧事随流水，但寒烟衰草凝绿。至今商女，时时犹唱，《后庭》遗曲。

【释文】

　　登高临远，举目远眺，正值故都的晚秋时节，天气开始变得肃杀萧索。清澈的长江水绵延千里，像一条白色绸绢；远处苍翠的山峰就像箭头耸立。来来往往的船只笼罩在一片夕阳的余晖里，西风掠过，酒店门前的大旗斜斜地竖立着。远处水天相接，淡淡的白云映照在水面，与水中行驶的船儿相映成趣。一眼望去，白鹭纷纷起舞，像是在银河上飞翔。这样的景致，就是用画也不足以呈现。

　　感叹往日，曾有多少人在此处争相过着豪华奢靡的生活。而他们最终也都如陈朝为隋军所灭那样，相继亡国，悲痛和悔恨连续不断。千百年来，人们登高远望，面对这壮丽的河山，徒然感叹世事

16. "Fragrance of Cinnamon Twigs" (I make a climb to cast my eyes afar) by Wang Anshi

I make a climb to cast my eyes afar. It is the late autumn of ancient capital. The atmosphere begins to turn solemn. The limpid Yangtze river flowing across thousands of miles looks like a white ribbon; emerald peaks tower in piles. Sailboats come and go in the afterglow of the setting sun. Against the western wind, wine shop streamers stand aslant. Colorful boats and clouds are pale; egrets rise over starry river. No painting could do justice to such a scene.

Recollect the bygone days, when people compete on grandeur and extravagance. Sigh for the scene beyond the city gates and atop the tower, sorrow and hatred come in succession. A thousand years on at this height, I sigh in vain for the glory and disgrace of the past. The old stories of the six dynasties are gone with the flowing water. Only the chilly mists and withered grasses remain green. Even the courtesans of this day still sing, from time to time, the old song of "Backyard."

兴衰荣辱。六朝的兴亡旧事已经像流水一样消逝了,只剩下寒凉的烟雾笼罩着衰败的荒草,呈现出一片暗绿色。而那些卖唱的歌女,也还在不时地唱着《后庭花》这样的亡国之曲。

【解析】

　　黄昇《花庵词选》将这首词题作"金陵怀古",上片写登楼远望,目之所及的金陵景致,下片通过怀古,揭露了六朝统治者奢靡的生活以及由此带来的衰亡。写景和抒怀恰当融合,境界雄浑阔大,是怀古之作中的名篇。

【 Commentary 】

In Huang Sheng (?) 's *Hua An's Selections of Song Lyrics,* this lyric is preserved with the title "Thoughts on the Past at Jinling". The first half writes about the poet who ascends the tower and looks into the distance. What he observes is the scenery of Jinling. The second half reveals the reason for the downfall of the Six (222-589) dynasties: the extravagant lifestyle of the rulers. This song combines scenery description and lyrical expression. It also brings a sense of historical sublimity. No wonder it has been well-circulated as a famous piece concerning the meditation on the past.

南詞新譜

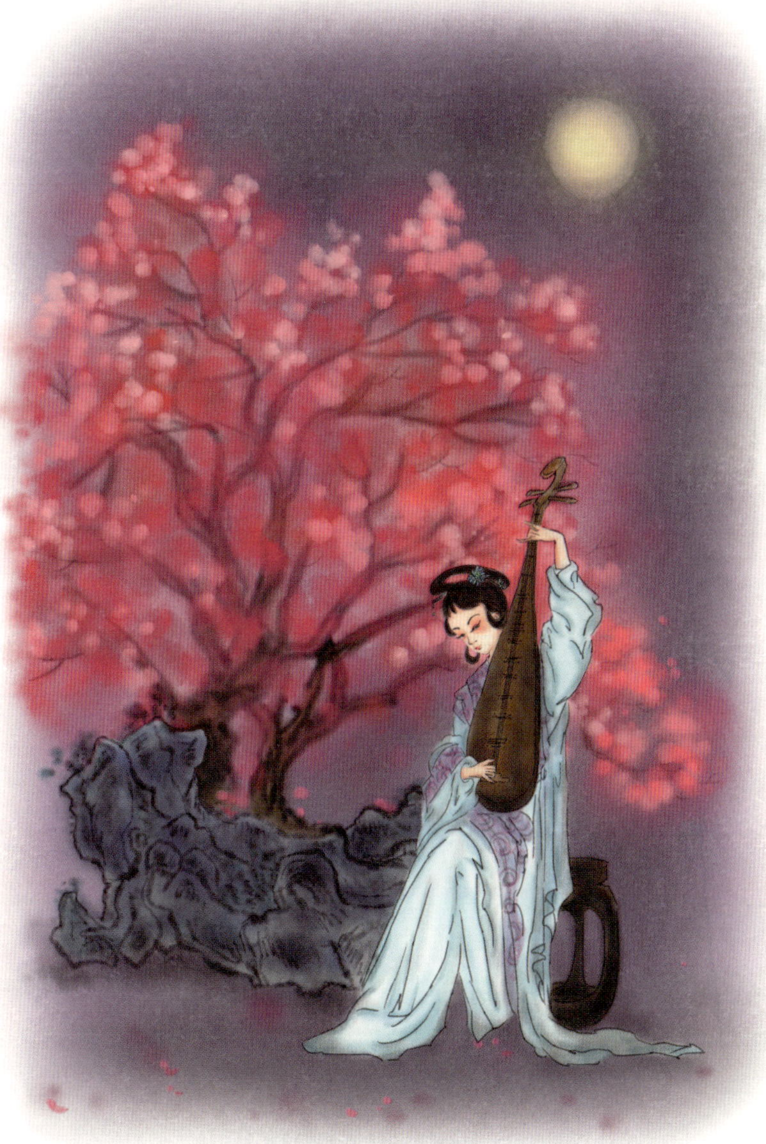

17. 晏几道《临江仙·梦后楼台高锁》

【原文】

梦后楼台高锁,酒醒帘幕低垂。去年春恨却来时,落花人独立,微雨燕双飞。

记得小蘋初见,两重心字罗衣,琵琶弦上说相思。当时明月在,曾照彩云归。

【释文】

从睡梦里、酒醉中醒来,只见楼台紧锁、帘幕低垂,早已是人去楼空。而此时,去年春天的离别之愁却又袭上心头,那时在寂寞的落花和蒙蒙的细雨中,只有我独自伫立,眼见燕儿在双双飞逐。

还记得初次见到小蘋,她正穿着绣有重叠的心字图案的衣衫,弹着琵琶,诉说着相思之情。当时曾照着小蘋归去的明月还在眼前,而小蘋的身影,早已无法寻觅。

【解析】

这首词为词人怀念歌女小蘋所作。上片写小蘋离去后人去楼空的寂寥景象,以及由此引起的伤春的情绪。"落花人独立,微雨燕双飞"二句直接套用前人诗句而有化腐朽为神奇之功。下片追忆初见小蘋时的情景,表现了对往日情事的回忆,全词笼罩着一种物是人非的怅惘之情。

17. "Immortal at Riverside" (I wake up from a dream, and the high tower is locked)
by Yan Jidao

I wake up from a dream, and the high tower is locked. I recover from intoxication, and the curtains are hanging low. The spring grief of last year seems to come. The flowers are falling and I stand alone. In a light rain, a pair of swallows flies.

I still remember when I first saw Petite Ping, who was in a silken dress embroidered with two hearts in a ring. She confided her lovesickness to the strings of pipa. The moon is as bright as then, and it shined on the returning rosy clouds.

【 Commentary 】

This lyric was written in honor of a courtesan Petite Ping. The first half describes the desolate scene after Ping passes away, by which the melancholic feelings for the passage of spring are aroused. The last two lines of the first stanza are not just a simple appropriation of former lines, for they provide rich meanings in the new context. The poet recalls his memory when he firstly met Ping in the second stanza. The whole song brings a gloomy sense of desolation and loss: everything is still there, but Ping is no longer present.

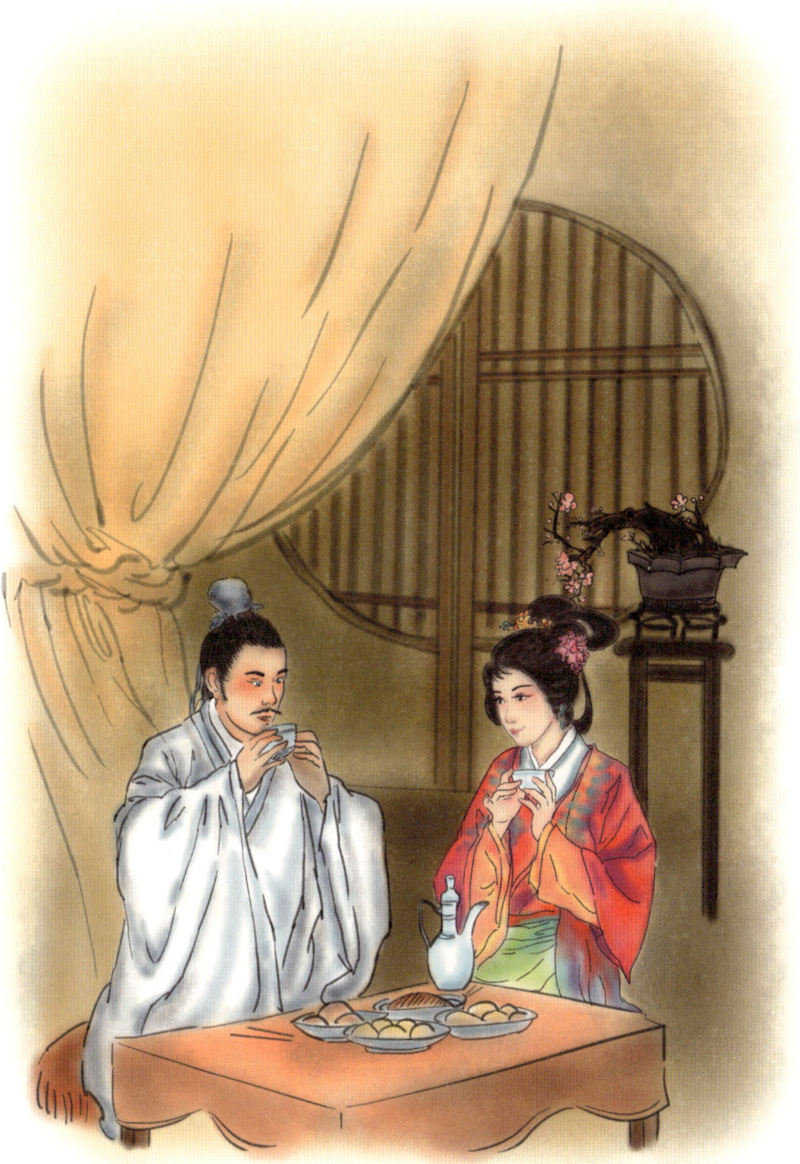

18. 晏几道《鹧鸪天·彩袖殷勤捧玉钟》

【原文】

　　彩袖殷勤捧玉钟,当年拚却醉颜红。舞低杨柳楼心月,歌尽桃花扇底风。

　　从别后,忆相逢,几回魂梦与君同。今宵剩把银釭照,犹恐相逢是梦中。

【释文】

　　当年你抬起彩袖,手捧玉杯殷勤向我劝酒,我甘愿开怀畅饮,脸上也因酒醉而变红。我们欢歌起舞,直到楼顶的月亮沉下柳梢,桃花扇底的风似乎都要被扇尽。

　　自从那一别之后,我时时回忆我们相逢的美好时光,多少回梦中仍与你一起。而今晚,我尽力举起银灯细细地将你打量,却担心这次的相逢是在梦里面。

【解析】

　　这首词写词人与其爱恋的歌女久别重逢。词的上片写离别之前的欢饮达旦,似实却虚。下片分为两层,前三句写离别后的相思之苦,后两句写重逢时的喜悦,似梦却真。词情委婉华丽,形式工整,是脍炙人口的爱情词作。

18. "Partridge Sky" (The colorful sleeves cordially serve the jade bells) by Yan Jidao

    The colorful sleeves cordially served the jade bells. In those days, I drank merrily and was tipsy with red face. You danced till the moon over the towers sank below the poplars and willows; you sang till the peach flower fans exhausted the wind.

    Since separation, I thought of our reunion, and for several times met you in my dreams. Tonight, I must set the silver lamp aglow, for fear our reunion is in a dream.

【 Commentary 】

    The lyric writes about an reunion of the poet and the singing girl he falls in love with. In the first stanza, the poet recalls the parting scene in the past, and the realistic descriptions of the farewell dinner are but memories of the past. There are two parts in the second stanza. The first three lines focuses on the lovesickness since their separation, and the last two lines writes about the happy occasion of their reunion. These dreamlike lines actually are reflections of what occurred in reality. This love song is famous for its beautiful words, elegant style and perfect matching of the structural requirements.

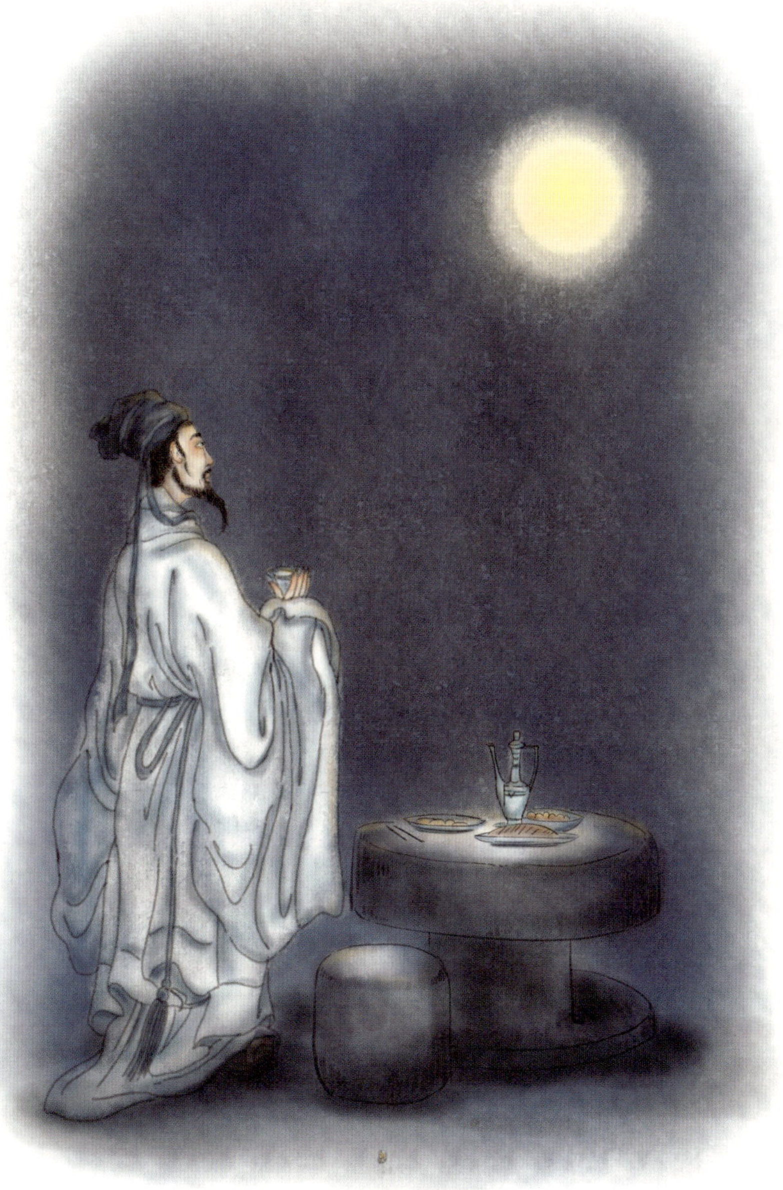

19. 苏轼《水调歌头·明月几时有》

【原文】

丙辰中秋,欢饮达旦,大醉,作此篇,兼怀子由。

明月几时有?把酒问青天。不知天上宫阙,今夕是何年。我欲乘风归去,又恐琼楼玉宇,高处不胜寒。起舞弄清影,何似在人间?

转朱阁,低绮户,照无眠。不应有恨,何事长向别时圆?人有悲欢离合,月有阴晴圆缺,此事古难全。但愿人长久,千里共婵娟。

【释文】

明月是从什么时候开始出现的?我举起酒杯遥问苍天。不知道天上的宫殿里,现在是何年何月。我想乘着清风回到那里,又害怕在那神仙居住的月中宫殿,禁受不住高耸九天而产生的寒冷。还是让我在月光下随着自己的身影一起起舞吧,天上哪有人间好呢?

月亮啊,转过了华丽的楼阁,又低低地照进雕花的门窗里,照着心事重重不能安眠的人。月亮啊,你是不应该对人有恨的,为什么总是在人们离别的时候变圆呢?人难免有悲欢离合,正如月儿有阴晴圆缺一样,这种事情自古以来就难以圆满。只希望人们能长久地活在世上,即使相隔千里,也能共同享受这美好的月色。

19. "Prelude to Water Melody" (How long will the bright moon appear) by Su Shi

How long will the bright moon appear? Holding a wine cup, I ask the blue sky. I do not know, in the celestial palaces, what time of the year would be tonight. I desire to ride the wind and go there, yet I am afraid the crystalline towers and jade palaces in the high place are too cold for me to bear. Rise and dance; play with the clear shadow. It does not seem like the human world.

Go around the vermillion mansions, stoops to the silk-pad doors, and shines on the sleepless. Bearing no grudge, why does the moon turn full when people are apart? Men have sorrows and joys, partings and reunions. The moon is dim or bright, and does wax and wane. There has been nothing perfect since the ancient time. I wish that man will live as long as they can. Though one thousand miles apart, we could still share the beauty of the moon together.

【解析】

　　这首词乃词人作于中秋之时的作品,其时苏轼与弟弟苏辙分别已久。欢度佳节的愉快和对弟弟的牵挂之情是这首词的基调。全篇围绕明月展开想象和思考,同时融入了对人世间悲欢离合的追问,体现了词人能够不拘于离愁别恨的旷达思想。

【 Commentary 】

This lyric was written by the famous poet Su Shi (1036-1101) at the time of the Mid-Autumn Day. He and his younger brother Su Zhe (1039-1112) had separated from each other for long. It is natural that he concerns his brother at this happy occasion for reunion. The poet's imagination and thoughts are around the image of the moon. Besides, this lyric touches upon the themes of reunion and separation in the human world, and also shows that the broad-minded poet is not attached to parting grief.

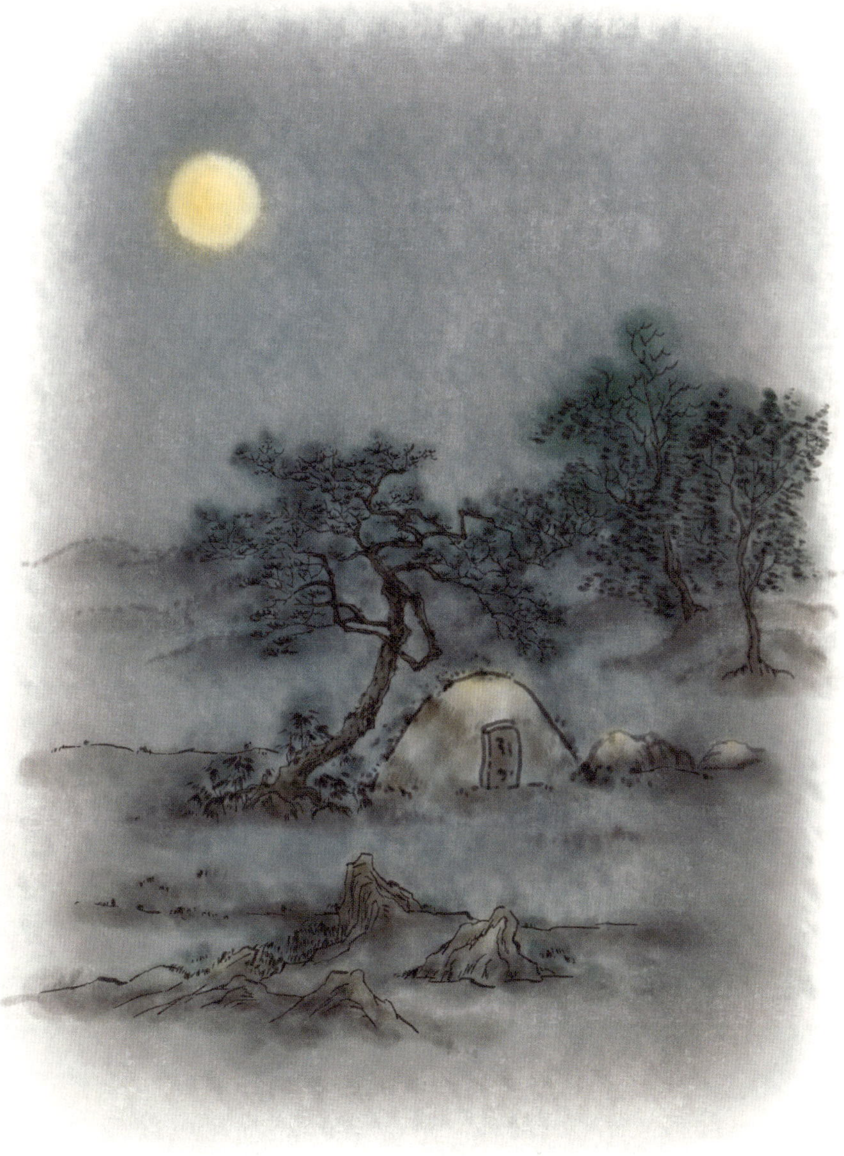

20. 苏轼《江城子·十年生死两茫茫》
乙卯正月二十日夜记梦

【原文】

　　十年生死两茫茫，不思量，自难忘。千里孤坟，无处话凄凉。纵使相逢应不识，尘满面，鬓如霜。

　　夜来幽梦忽还乡，小轩窗，正梳妆。相顾无言，惟有泪千行。料得年年肠断处，明月夜，短松冈。

【释文】

　　你我生死两隔，茫然不知彼此的情况已有十年，纵然我不去想念你，也终究难以忘怀过去的岁月。而你的坟茔在千里之外孤单地立着，凄凉之境无处可以诉说。即使相逢，你应该也不认识我了，我已是风尘满面，两鬓白如秋霜。

　　昨夜做梦忽然回到了家乡，你正坐在小屋的窗前梳妆打扮。你我相对，一句话都没说，只有眼泪簌簌而下。想来那伤心之处，年复一年，都只有夜间的明月照着种有矮小松树的山冈。

【解析】

　　这首词为词人在妻子逝世十年之时，所作的一首悼念亡妻的作品。上片实写词人对其妻的思念之情，下片虚写梦境，加深全词的悲伤基调。词中使用白描手法，语言朴素，但感情却深沉悲切。

20. "River Town" (For ten years, the living and the dead are both in ignorance of each other) by Su Shi
Record of My Dream on the Twentieth Night of the First Month in the *Yi Mao Year*

For ten years, the living and the dead are both in ignorance of each other. I try not to think of you, but how can I forget! a Lonely grave lies a thousand miles away, and there is nowhere to talk the deep sorrows out. Even if we meet again, you will not recognize me, for my face is full of dust and my temples resemble frost.

Last night, in a gloomy dream, I suddenly returned home. By the window of the little room, you were combing your hair and making up. We looked at each other, wordless, only a thousand lines of tears. I guess, year after year, the heartbreaking place is around short pine mound on moonlit nights.

【 Commentary 】

This mourning lyric was written by the poet to commemorate the 10th anniversary of his wife's death. The first stanza shows the poet misses his wife very much. The second stanza recalls his dream and this further increases the sorrows conveyed throughout the whole song. Though its language is simple and plain, the tone of the song is sincere and sorrowful.

南詞新譜

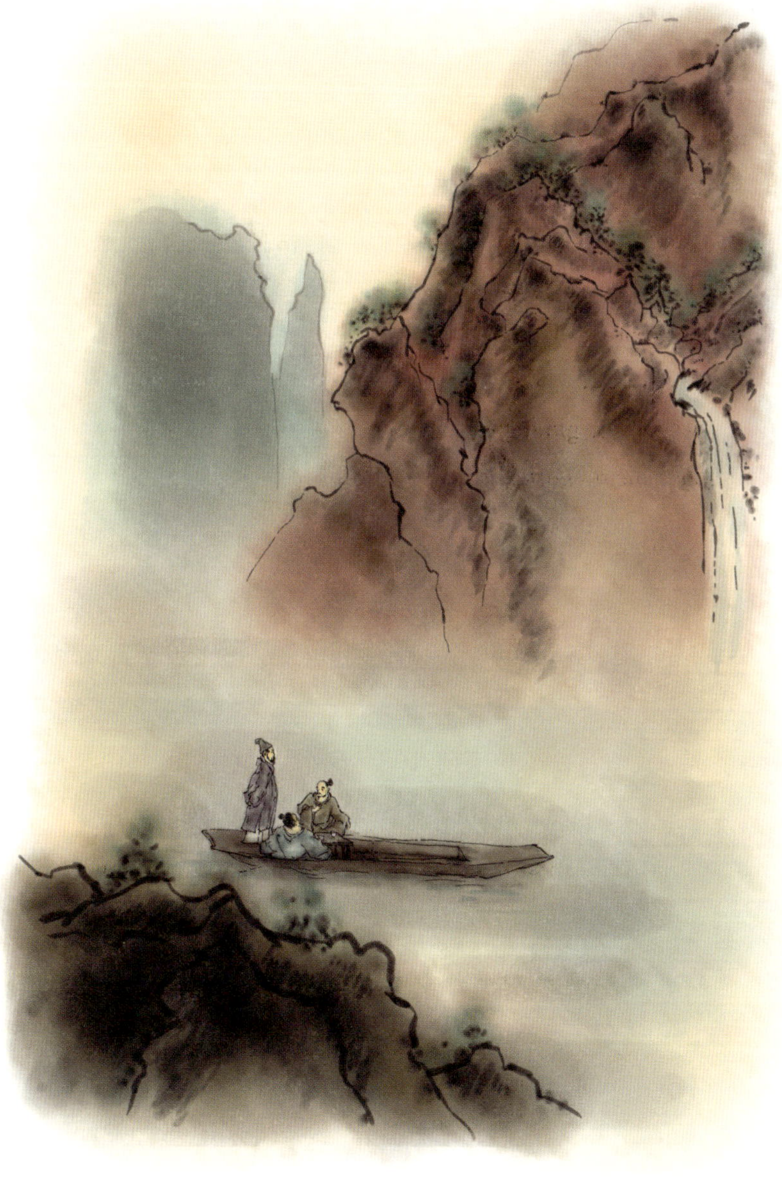

21. 苏轼《念奴娇·大江东去》
赤壁怀古

【原文】

　　大江东去,浪淘尽,千古风流人物。故垒西边,人道是,三国周郎赤壁。乱石穿空,惊涛拍岸,卷起千堆雪。江山如画,一时多少豪杰。

　　遥想公瑾当年,小乔初嫁了,雄姿英发。羽扇纶巾,谈笑间,樯橹灰飞烟灭。故国神游,多情应笑我,早生华发。人生如梦,一尊还酹江月。

【释文】

　　长江滚滚,向东流去,巨浪淘尽千百年来的英雄人物。旧时的营垒西边,据人们所说是三国时期周郎赤壁鏖战的地方。耸立的峭壁似要刺破天空,惊人的巨涛拍打着江岸,卷起的浪花像是千万堆的白雪。秀丽的江山像是一幅画卷,自古以来涌现了多少的英雄豪杰。

　　回想当年的公瑾,小乔刚刚嫁与他,那时的他多么英气勃发。手摇羽扇头戴纶巾,潇洒的谈笑之间,敌军的战船便被烧得灰飞烟灭。神思游历于故国之地,应该笑自己多情善感,早早地生出花白的头发。人生就像一场梦,且洒一杯酒祭奠江上的明月。

21. "Remembering the Pretty Maid" (The great river flows to the east) by Su Shi
Thoughts on the Past at Red Cliff

The great river flows to the east, and its billows sweep away the brilliant figures of a thousand generations. To the west of the old forts, people say, is Lord Zhou's Red Cliff in the period of the Three Kingdoms. Rugged rocks pierce into the sky; raging waves beat against the shore, rolling up a thousand piles of snow. The river and the mountains seem to form a picture, where once there were numerous heroes.

Recollect Lord Zhou in those years, when he newly married Petite Qiao. His valorous features were shown forth; with a feather fan and a silk head-crest; amid his talking and laughing, the enemy's ships turned into ashes and smoke. As my mind wandered in the old country, I should laugh at my sentimentality that caused my early grey hair. Human life is like a dream; with a cup of wine, allow me to pour a libation to the moon over the river.

【解析】

这首词乃苏轼谪居黄州期间的作品。分三个部分,第一部分写赤壁的壮阔之景;第二部分从景到人,写历史上的周郎其人以及他所立下的赫赫战功;第三部分由周郎而生感慨:人生如梦,华发早生而功业未成,实在是一件憾事。全词气势磅礴,刻画人物形象突出,写景、议论、抒情完美结合,乃作者的代表作品之一。

【 Commentary 】

This lyric was written by Su Shi when he was living in political exile at Huangzhou. There are three parts in this song. The first part describes the broad view of the Red Cliff. The second part moves from the scenery to the historical figure Zhou Yu (175-210) and his accomplishments. The third part conveys the poet's feelings toward history: life is like a dream; it is a pity when one gets old without any achievements. This is one of the most representative works by Su Shi, for it is featured by an embodiment of heroic spirit, outstanding depiction of images and a perfect combination of scenery, comments and lyrical expression.

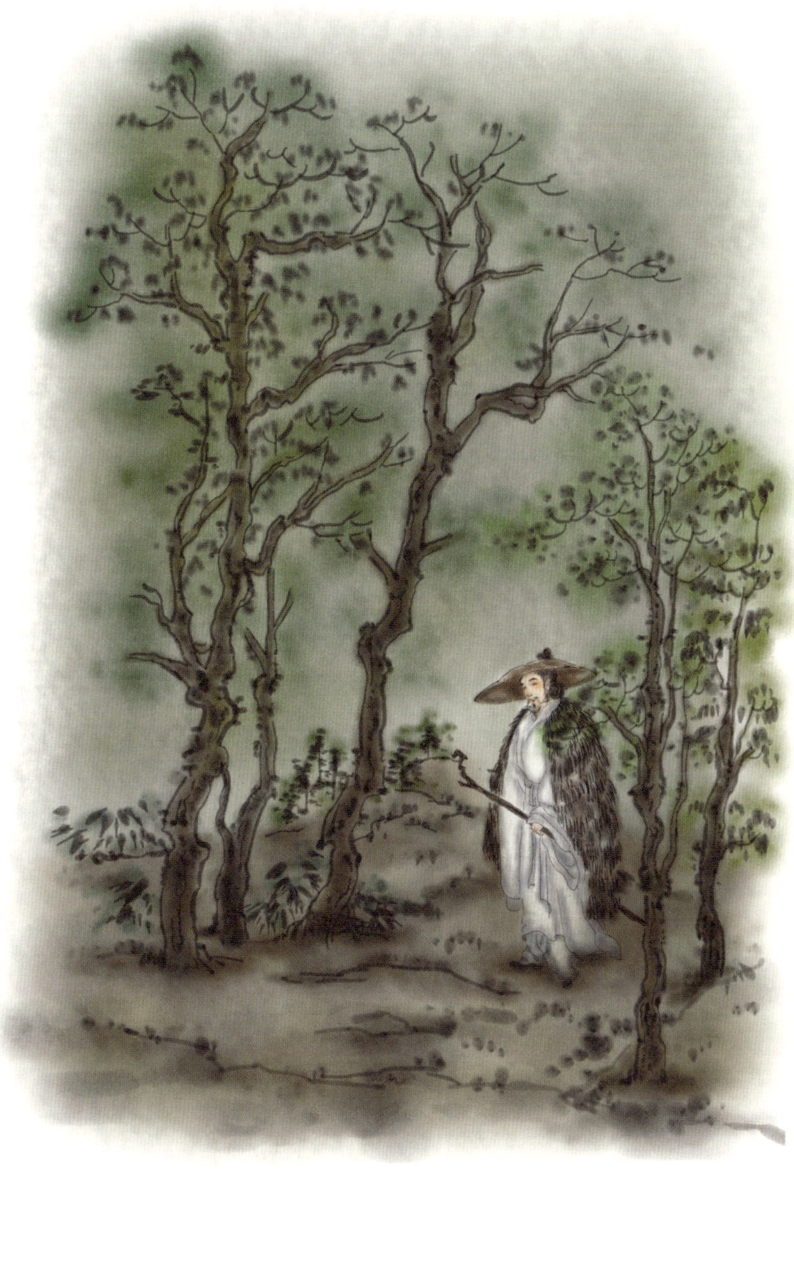

22. 苏轼《定风波·莫听穿林打叶声》

【原文】

三月七日沙湖道中遇雨。雨具先去，同行皆狼狈，余独不觉。已而遂晴。故作此。

莫听穿林打叶声，何妨吟啸且徐行。竹杖芒鞋轻胜马。谁怕？一蓑烟雨任平生。

料峭春风吹酒醒，微冷，山头斜照却相迎。回首向来萧瑟处，归去，也无风雨也无晴。

【释文】

不要去听那雨点透过树林打在树叶上的声音，不妨吟诗、长啸，缓步而行。拄着竹杖，踏着草鞋，比骑马而行还要轻便，有什么可怕的呢？披一件蓑衣，任凭风吹雨打，我也泰然处之。

带些许寒意的春风吹醒了我的酒意，身上微微感到有些冷，夕阳却刚好透过山头迎面照过来。回头看看刚才遇雨的地方，我继续信步向前，似乎这趟归程中既没有风雨也没有放晴。

【解析】

这首词所记乃苏轼在黄州之时，某次在野外归途中偶遇风雨这样一件生活小事。上片写雨至，下片写转晴，通过"同行皆狼狈，余独不觉"，来表现自己对于"晴"和"雨"的态度。整首词体现了词人旷达的襟怀。

22. "Calm the Waves" (Do not listen to the rain that rustles the woods and beats against the leaves) by Su Shi

Do not listen to the rain that rustles the woods and beats against the leaves. Why not sing and whistle, while walk slowly? A bamboo cane and sandals are lighter than horses. Who is afraid? A palm bark cape is enough for any misty rains in life.

The chilly spring wind sobers up the drunkenness, and it is a slight cold. The slanting sun over the mountains greets me. Looking back over the dreary beaten track, I return, indifferent to wind, rain or shine.

【 Commentary 】

This lyric was written by Su Shi when he was returning from a field trip on a rainy day at Huangzhou. The first stanza writes the arrival of the rain; the second stanza describes the sunny weather. The poet shows his attitude toward the conditions of "rainy" and "sunny" weather through the introductory line: "those who are in company with me all felt uncomfortable and awkward, but I did not feel so." The whole lyric shows that the poet is a broad-minded scholar who is free of care.

南峯詞話

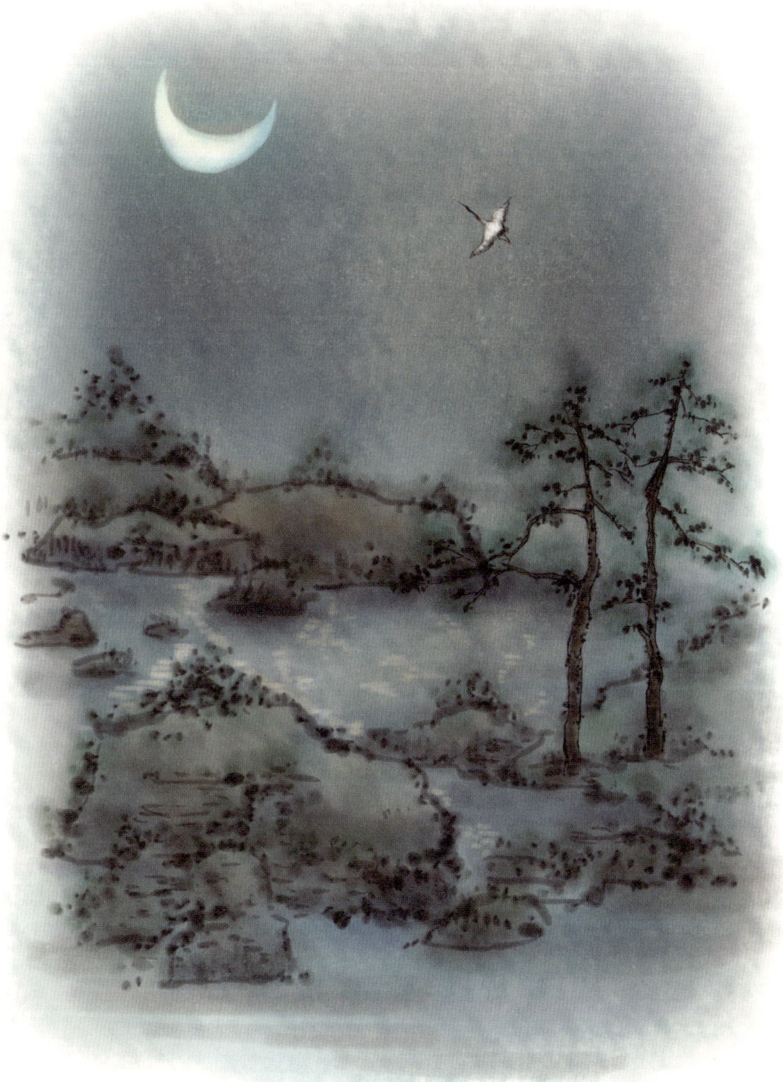

23. 苏轼《卜算子·缺月挂疏桐》
黄州定慧院寓居作

【原文】

缺月挂疏桐,漏断人初静。谁见幽人独往来,缥缈孤鸿影。惊起却回头,有恨无人省。拣尽寒枝不肯栖,寂寞沙洲冷。

【释文】

残月高高地挂在稀疏的梧桐树上,漏壶的水渐少(滴漏声已很难听到),四周已是一片寂静。难道还有幽居的人在独自往来?原来是那若有若无的孤雁的身影。

(大雁)受惊飞起,然而又回头看看,心中有悲愁却无人知晓。它挑选遍了冬日里的树枝也不肯栖息下来,宁愿留在那寂寞寒冷的沙洲之上。

【解析】

这首词以孤雁自喻,上片写黄州定慧院的夜景,引出孤雁;下片以孤雁不愿攀援高枝,宁愿与冰冷寂寞的沙洲为伴,表现了词人自身不愿与时俗同流的志向。

23. "Divination" (The waning moon hangs over the sparse wutong tree) by Su Shi
Composed while staying at the Dinghui Monastery in Huangzhou

The waning moon hangs over the sparse wutong tree. The clepsydras are still and human voices become silent. Who sees a hermit coming and going all alone? The shadow of a lonely goose is in misty sky.

Startled, it suddenly turns back, with its woe that no one knows. It chooses no chilly branches to perch on, but a lonely and cold sandbank.

【 Commentary 】

In this lyric, the poet likens himself to a lonely goose. The first half describes the night scene of the Dinghui Monastery at Huangzhou so as to lead to the image of the lonely swan. The second half writes about a lonely goose that refuses to perch on a high branch. Instead, it prefers to befriend the cold islet. And the lyric also reflects the poet refuses to associate himself with evil elements.

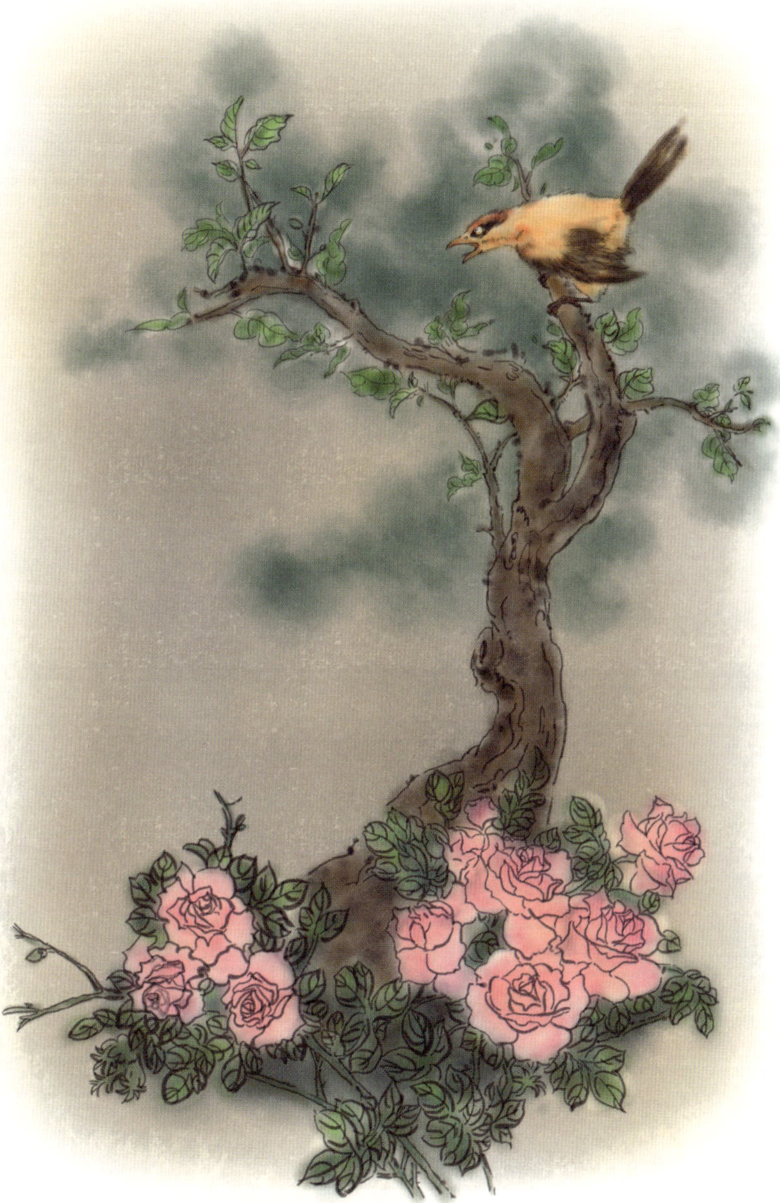

24. 黄庭坚《清平乐·春归何处》

【原文】

春归何处？寂寞无行路。若有人知春去处，唤取归来同住。

春无踪迹谁知？除非问取黄鹂。百啭无人能解，因风飞过蔷薇。

【释文】

春天回到哪里？四周一片清寂，已经看不见它的踪迹。假如有人知道春天的去处，请唤春回来和我们住在一起。

春天一去没有踪迹，有谁知道它去了什么地方呢？（要想知道）除非问一问那树上的黄鹂鸟。然而虽然那黄鹂一遍遍地婉转啼鸣，却没有人能懂得它的意思。只见它乘着风势，飞过盛开的蔷薇。

【解析】

这首词表现了词人惜春、恋春的情怀。全篇运用朴素直白的口语和拟人化的方式，通过问答的形式，巧妙地表现了词人对"春去也"的惋惜。

24. "Pure Serene Music" (Where has spring gone) by Huang Tingjian

Where has spring gone? Lonely, no trace left. If anyone knows where spring goes, call her to come back and stay with us.

Spring leaves no trace, and who knows where? Unless you ask a yellow oriole. But no one can explain its chirps. Riding the wind, it flies over the roses.

【 Commentary 】

The poet conveys his sympathy and affection to the spring season in this lyric. Its language is simple, direct and colloquial. The devices of personification, questions and answers uniquely show the poet's sympathetic feelings for the passage of spring.

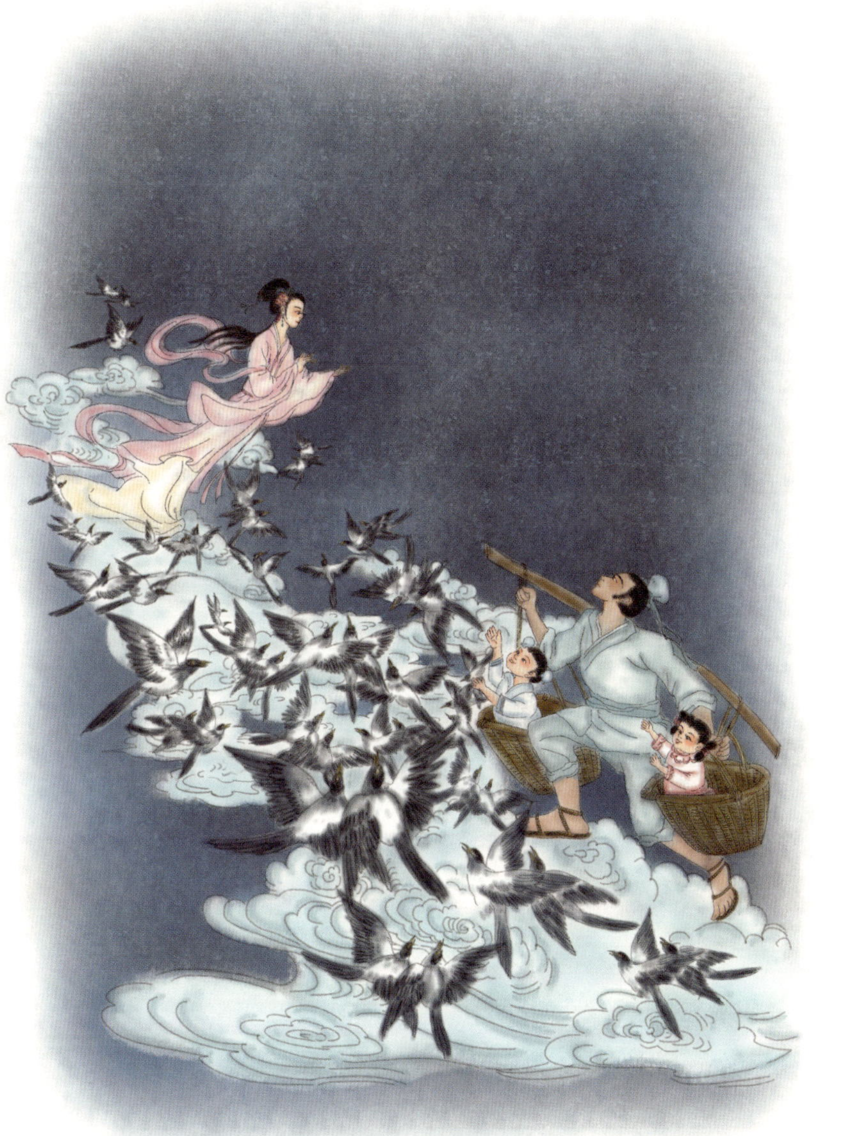

25. 秦观《鹊桥仙·纤云弄巧》

【原文】

纤云弄巧,飞星传恨,银汉迢迢暗度。金风玉露一相逢,便胜却人间无数。

柔情似水,佳期如梦,忍顾鹊桥归路。两情若是久长时,又岂在朝朝暮暮。

【释文】

纤薄的云彩变幻出各种巧妙的花样,牵牛、织女二星隔着银河相对,传递着不得相聚的憾恨。只有在今日(七月七日),他们才能在暗夜里渡过辽阔的天河相会。(而他们)在这秋风、白露初降之日的一次美好相逢,就胜过了人间夫妇无数次的聚会。

当此之时,脉脉的柔情如水,欢会的时光像梦,怎么忍心回顾那条从鹊桥回去的路呢?两人的爱情如果能地久天长,何必在乎是不是时时相守呢!

【解析】

这首词根据魏晋以来流传甚广的牛郎织女的故事改写而成,在写出恋爱双方的离合悲欢之情的同时,能够推出新意,"两情若是久长时,又岂在朝朝暮暮",即真正的爱情能够经历时间和空间的考验,即使终年天各一方,也能胜过一些庸俗的朝夕相对。

25. "Magpie Bridge Immortal" (Slender clouds display delicate shapes) by Qin Guan

Slender clouds display delicate shapes; flying stars pass on regrets. They secretly cross the far off Milky Way. Amid the golden wind and jade dew, they meet, and this meeting surpasses countless reunions in human world.

The tender affection is like water; the happy occasion is like a dream. How unbearable to see the returning way on the Magpie Bridge! If love between both means to be lasting for long, why should they stay together day and night?

【 Commentary 】

This lyric is based on the folk tale of the Cowherd and the Weaver Girl, and the tale has been widely circulated since the Wei and Jin (220-420) dynasties. The poet writes about the feelings of reunions and separations on both sides, and he provides a new perspective in the last couplet: true love meant to be eternal will transcend the limitation of time and space. Though the Cowherd and the Weaver Girl are separated from each other all year long, their love surpasses the lovers who stay together day and night in human world.

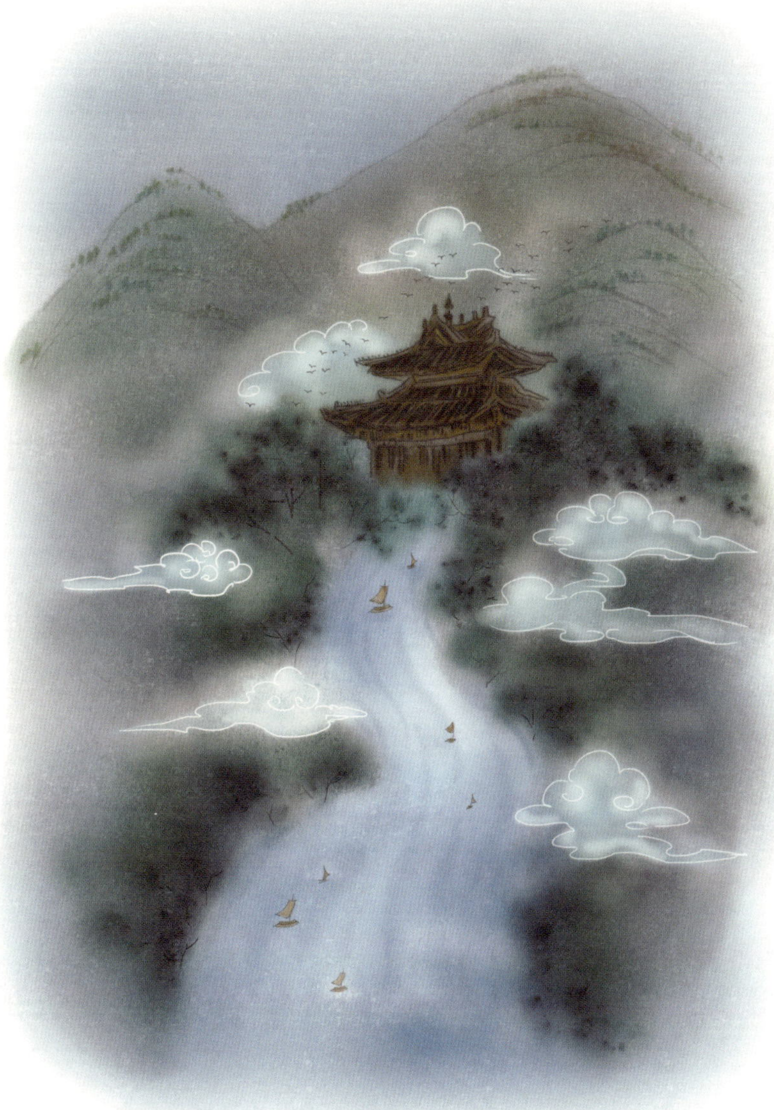

26. 秦观《踏莎行·雾失楼台》
郴州旅舍

【原文】

雾失楼台,月迷津渡,桃源望断无寻处。可堪孤馆闭春寒,杜鹃声里斜阳暮。

驿寄梅花,鱼传尺素,砌成此恨无重数。郴江幸自绕郴山,为谁流下潇湘去?

【释文】

楼台消失在夜雾中,渡口也在朦胧的月色中迷失了。而我所处的郴州,虽然地近桃源,却已无法寻觅当时的乐土。怎能忍受独自幽闭在客馆、春寒料峭,听着杜鹃凄厉的啼鸣直到夕阳西下、暮色昏昏?

远方的朋友,传来了音讯,寄来了温暖的安慰,然而却使我平添了数不尽的离恨。郴江啊,你本来是环绕着郴山的,为什么要向潇湘流去呢?

【解析】

这首词作于词人被贬谪郴州时,词人以凄婉的笔调,描写了谪居之地的孤寂荒凉,表现了失意之后的苦闷和哀怨。相传,有同样贬谪遭遇的苏轼极爱最后两句,曾赞赏不已并题于扇子上。

26. "Treading on Grass" (Towers and terraces are lost in mist) by Qin Guan
At an Inn in *Chenzhou*

Towers and terraces are lost in mist. Ferry is dim in moonlight. I look for the Dale of Peach Blossom and it is nowhere to be found. How can I bear the spring cold in a lonely closed inn? At dusk, the cuckoos are crying and the sun is setting.

The mume flowers sent by post, and the letters brought by fish, pile up countless layers of grief. The Chen River should have been around the Chen Mountain, why does it flow down to join the Xiang river?

【 Commentary 】

This lyric was written by the poet when he was demoted to Chenzhou. The poet describes a desolate and solitary place where he lives after the official exile and expresses his sorrowful feelings of being in a state of unfulfillment. It was said that the famous poet Su Shi (1036-1101), who had similar experience, loved the last couplet so much that he wrote them on his own fan.

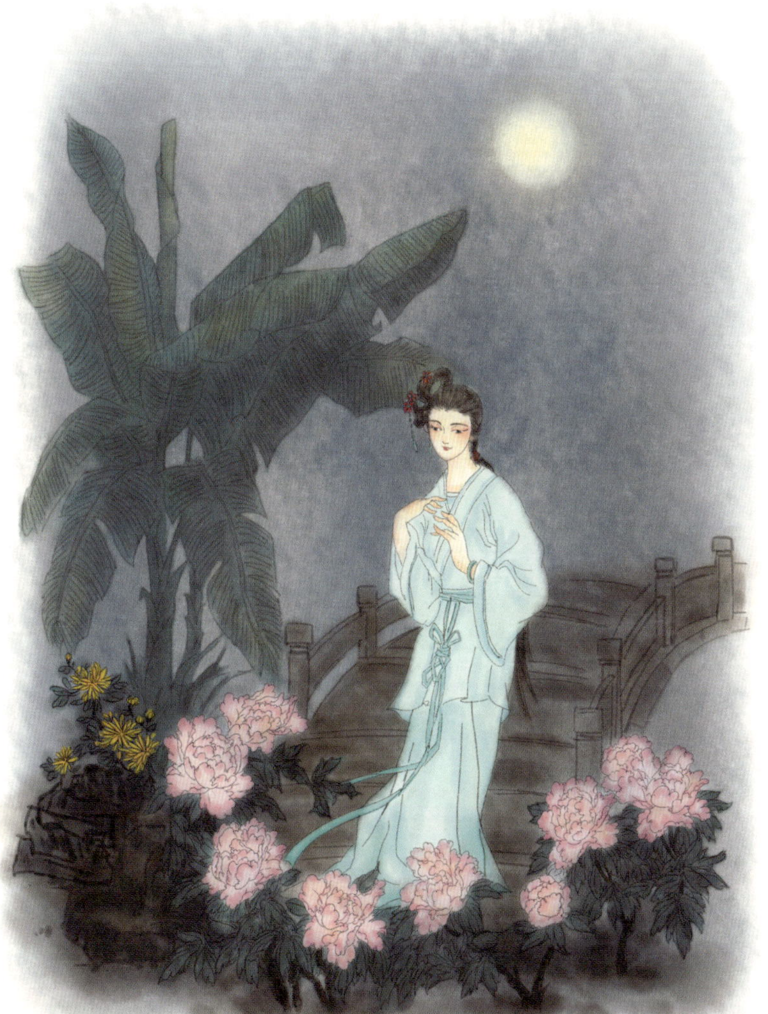

27. 贺铸《青玉案·凌波不过横塘路》

【原文】

　　凌波不过横塘路。但目送、芳尘去。锦瑟华年谁与度？月桥花院，琐窗朱户。只有春知处。

　　飞云冉冉蘅皋暮。彩笔新题断肠句。试问闲愁都几许？一川烟草，满城风絮。梅子黄时雨。

【释文】

　　姑娘那轻盈的步子并没有踏入横塘路这边，我只好默默地目送她远去。她那美好的青春岁月是与谁共同度过的呢？是在那月光下、小桥边、种满花的庭院里，还是在那有着雕花的窗户和朱红的大门内？大概只有春天知道她在哪里。

　　浮云在天空中缓缓地流动，长满香草的河岸边暮色已经降临。我手执一杆五色笔，新写成令人断肠的诗句。若是问我无故的愁绪有多少，正如那遍地青烟似的芳草、满城飞舞的柳絮，还有那黄梅时节连绵不断的阴雨。

27. "Green Jade Table" (Her graceful steps are not across the Road of Horizontal Pond) by He Zhu

Her graceful steps are not across the Road of Horizontal Pond. But I follow her with my eyes as the fragrant dusts arise. With whom she will spend her youthful days, on a crescent-shaped bridge, in a garden full of flowers, or behind the patterned windows and vermilion doors? Only spring knows the place.

Clouds are floating on and on, and dusk is approaching the fragrant-grass plain. With a color brush, I wrote new lines of heartbroken verse. How much, you may ask, idle grief is there in total? A river of misty grass, a townful of catkins in the wind, and the rain when plums turn yellow.

【解析】

　　这首词以词人的相思之情起笔,"凌波""芳尘"写词人所见的这位体态轻盈的女子。然而词人对其毫无所知,只能凭想象猜测她的住处。住处的华丽以及"只有春知处"的臆测越发显现出其人的寂寞。下片通过相思之情的渲染转入对闲愁的表达,连用三个具体的复合型物象,独出心裁地将抽象的、无迹可求的"闲愁"表达出来。而这些物象本身也构成了一幅美丽的江南梅雨时节的图景,因此颇受赞誉。贺铸也因此得名,被称为"贺梅子"。

【 Commentary 】

This lyric begins with the poet's yearning for love. "Graceful steps" and "fragrant dusts" are vivid words that indirectly describe the slim figure of the lady the poet saw. Nonetheless, the poet knows nothing about the lady, so he could only guess at her whereabouts. The various assumptions and the line "only spring knows the place" highlight the fact that the poet is all alone. The second half concentrates on the expression of idle grief. The three metaphors in the end creatively answer the question and present specific images for the abstract "idle grief". And these images form a beautiful picture of a raining season in southern China. No wonder the song has been widely praised. Because of this lyric, He Zhu acquired another name as "Plum He".

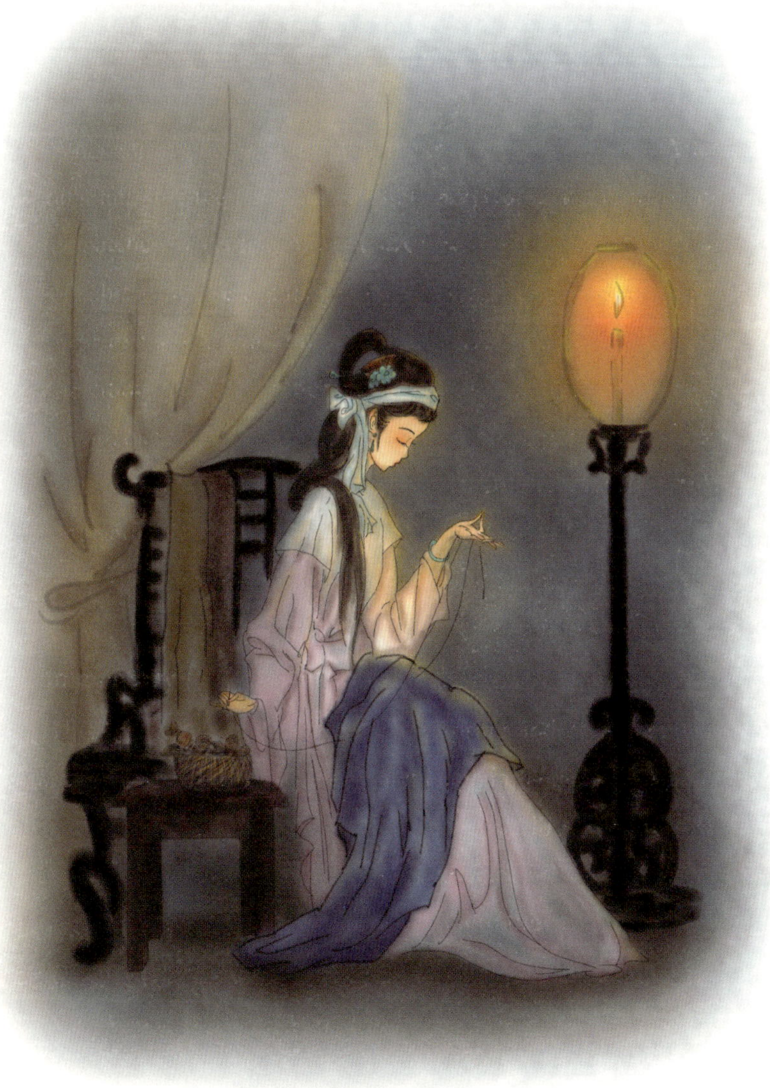

28. 贺铸《鹧鸪天·重过阊门万事非》

【原文】

重过阊门万事非,同来何事不同归?梧桐半死清霜后,头白鸳鸯失伴飞。

原上草,露初晞,旧栖新垄两依依。空床卧听南窗雨,谁复挑灯夜补衣?

【释文】

再次路过苏州阊门,这里已人事全非。你我一同前来,为何不能一同归去?现在的我,正如遭受霜打后半死半生的梧桐,又像是白头失伴、独自飞去的鸳鸯。

原野上的青草,露珠刚刚被晒干。而无论是我们的旧居,还是你的新坟,都让我徘徊良久,不忍离去。如今,躺在空空的床上听着窗外的雨声,还有谁会再为我深夜挑灯,缝补衣裳呢?

【解析】

这是词人悼念其亡妻的作品。有宋一代,在诸多描写爱情的词中,写给伶人歌妓的作品不少,但写给妻子的作品并不多。而词人贺铸与他的妻子一起经历了生活的艰辛,感情甚深,其妻死后,词人重游故地,心生感慨,写下了这首著名的悼亡之作。

28. "Partridge Sky" (I pass Chang Gate again, but everything is different)
by He Zhu

I pass Chang Gate again, but everything is different. We came out together; why we cannot go back together? I am like a wutong tree, half dead after pure frost, or a white-headed mandarin duck, flying without its mate.

Grass is on the plain and dew is just dry. I linger on and on, between the old residence and the new grave. On an empty bed, I lie and listen to the rainfall from the southern window. Who would trim the wick and mend the clothes now?

【 Commentary 】

This is a mourning lyric for the poet's dead wife. Love songs and poems abounded in the Song dynasty (960-1297), and many of them were written for courtesans, but very few were for wives. The poet and his wife went through thick and thin for many years. After his wife died, He Zhu revisited the place where they had spent enjoyable time together and this experience recalled his memories. Hence, he completed this famous lyric of lamentation.

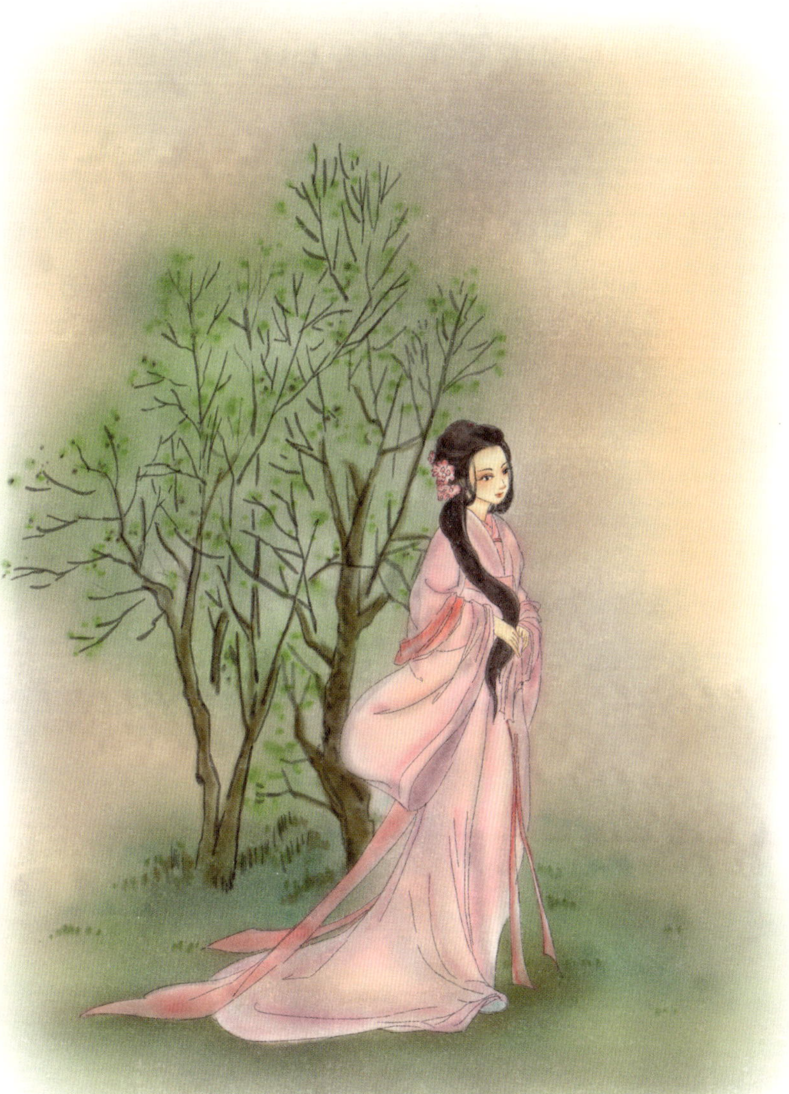

29. 王观《卜算子·水是眼波横》
送鲍浩然之浙东

【原文】

水是眼波横,山是眉峰聚。欲问行人去那边?眉眼盈盈处。
才始送春归,又送君归去。若到江南赶上春,千万和春住。

【释文】

流水如那美人的眼波横流,山峰如美人的眉峰攒聚。想要问行人去哪里,正是那山明水秀之地。

刚刚送走了春天,又要送你归去。要是你到江南还能赶上春天,千万要和她一块儿停下脚步。

【解析】

这是一首送别友人的词。词的上片以眼喻水、以眉喻山,语带双关、构思巧妙。下片写别绪的同时抒发了对春日的留恋,惜别和惜春的感情都含蓄地体现了出来。

29. "Divination" (The waters are the waves across the eyes) by Wang Guan
Seeing off Bao Haoran for Zhedong

The waters are the waves across the eyes, and the hills are the gathered brow peaks. You may ask, where are the travelers going? To the fine place of eyes and brows.

I have just sent spring away, now I am seeing you off. If you catch up with spring in the south, you keep it there by all means.

【 Commentary 】

This lyric is about bidding a farewell to a friend. In the first half, eyes and brows are likened to rivers and hills respectively. The puns the poet used in it are very impressive and ingenious. While writing about the feelings of separation, the poet also expresses his affection for spring in the second stanza. These delicate emotions are all embodied in the verses.

南懷瑾選集

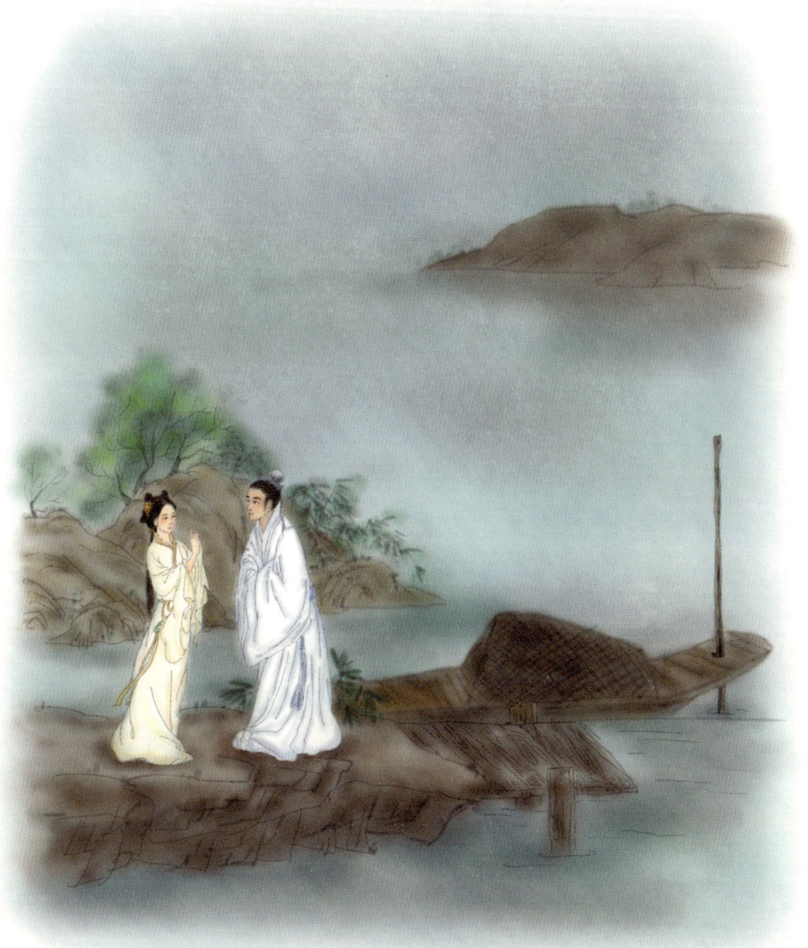

30. 李之仪《卜算子·我住长江头》

【原文】

我住长江头,君住长江尾。日日思君不见君,共饮长江水。此水几时休,此恨何时已?只愿君心似我心,定不负相思意。

【释文】

我住在长江的上游,你住在长江的末端。天天思念着你却又见不到你,虽然你我都喝着长江的水。

这流水何时才能停止,这遗恨何时才能罢休?只希望你的心能和我的心一样,那么,就不会辜负这互相思念的心意。

【解析】

这是一首具有民歌特色的小令。上片借长江起兴,突出"日日思君不见君"这一情感主题。下片转入抒情,承上思君不见,进一步抒写别恨。结尾两句则既表明了自己的心意,也是对两人关系的期许。全词以江水为抒情线索,写恋情极有情致。

30. "Divination" (I live upstream of the Yangtze) by Li Zhiyi

I live upstream of the Yangtze, and you live downstream of the Yangtze. Day after day, I long for you but I see you not, though we both drink from the Yangtze.

When will this water cease to run? When will this regret end? I only hope that your heart would be like mine, and we must never be unworthy of our mutual affections.

【 Commentary 】

This piece of work possesses a strong feature of Chinese folk songs. The first stanza starts with the Yangtze, and focuses on "Day after day, I long for you but I see you not." The second stanza continues with the emphasis on parting grief. The last couplet speaks out the poet's own wish and the expectation for their future. The "river" is the thread woven in the whole piece which is an excellent love song.

南詞敘錄

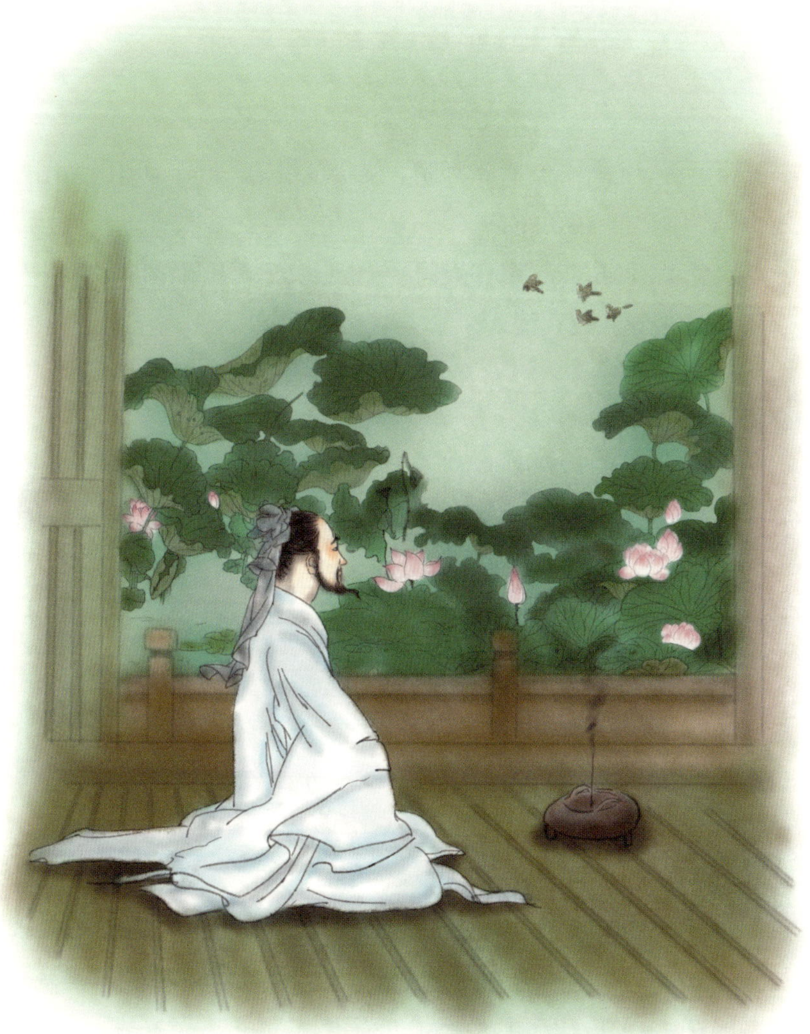

31. 周邦彦《苏幕遮·燎沉香》

【原文】

燎沉香,消溽暑。鸟雀呼晴,侵晓窥檐语。叶上初阳干宿雨,水面清圆,一一风荷举。

故乡遥,何日去?家住吴门,久作长安旅。五月渔郎相忆否?小楫轻舟,梦入芙蓉浦。

【释文】

焚起沉香,来消除夏天潮湿的暑气。鸟雀叽叽喳喳地呼唤着晴天,大清早便在屋檐下边东张西望,边交头接耳。初升的太阳映照在荷叶上,晒干了昨夜的雨,水面上青翠圆润的荷叶,似乎在晨风中一张张擎举着。

此情此景,使我想到路途遥远的故乡,不知何时才能归去?我家本在吴越,却长久地客居京城。五月,家乡一起嬉戏钓鱼的旧伴不知道是否还记得我?而我只能在梦里,划着小船来到旧时的荷花塘。

【解析】

这首词上片写雨后初晴之景,太阳升起,荷叶青翠圆润,在水面上摇曳生姿。"清圆"写出了荷的体态,"举"字则写出了荷花的动态之美。下片由眼前之景思及自身的状况,长久客居的我,只能在梦中回到故乡。江南五月的秀丽风光在此词中得到了有力的展现。

31. "Screened by Southern Curtain" (Burning the eaglewood incense) by Zhou Bangyan

Burning the eaglewood incense, to temper the sultry summer heat. Birds and sparrows are calling a sunny day; at dawn, they are peeping out under the eaves and chirping. The early sun over the leaves dries the overnight rain. The leaves are fresh and round on water surface. One by one, the lotus leaves stand up in breeze.

My hometown is far away; what day to return? My home is in Wu Gate, but for long I am a traveler in Chang'an. In May, will the fishing friend remember me or not? In a light boat with small oars, I sail to Lotus Flower Pond in dream.

【Commentary】

The first stanza writes about the clear day after the rain: the sun rises; the lotus leaves are green and round, swinging with the wind and displaying graceful poses on water. The characters "fresh and round" outline the shape of the lotus leaves and the phrase "stand up" shows the beauty of the lotus leaves swaying in the wind. The second stanza moves from the scenery to the poet himself: a stranger traveling in a foreign place who can only return home in the dream. The beautiful scenery of southern China is vividly represented in the lyric.

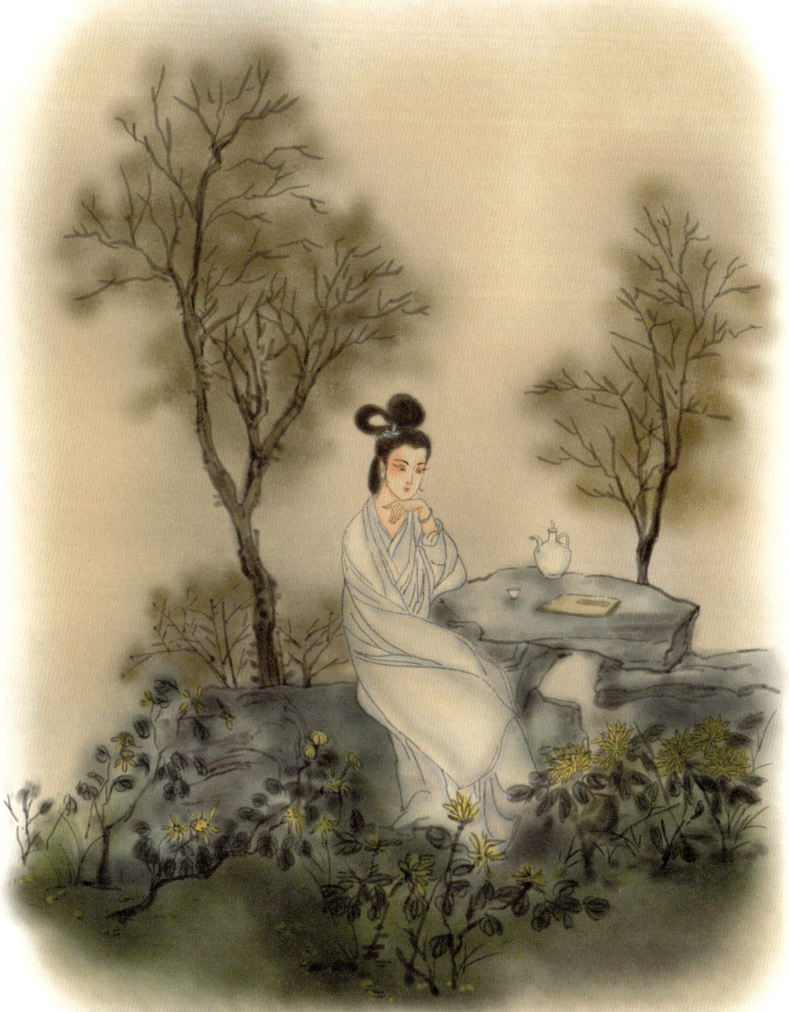

32. 李清照《醉花阴·薄雾浓云愁永昼》

【原文】

薄雾浓云愁永昼,瑞脑消金兽。佳节又重阳,玉枕纱厨,半夜凉初透。

东篱把酒黄昏后,有暗香盈袖。莫道不消魂,帘卷西风,人比黄花瘦。

【释文】

铜香炉中焚着瑞脑香,而这烟气忽浓忽淡,使我一整日都愁眉不展,只恨白日太长。又到了重阳佳节,枕着玉枕睡在纱帐中,到半夜已能感觉到微微的凉意。

黄昏以后,在菊花篱旁饮酒,有隐隐的香气袭来,沾满衫袖。别说此情此景不让人伤神,看那西风卷起帘幕,帘内的人儿简直比菊花还要消瘦。

【解析】

这首词乃记词人在秋日重阳之时把酒赏菊,然而却难以排遣内心的愁闷。结尾三句,在帘幕被西风卷起的萧瑟气氛中,将人与黄花对比,一"瘦"字,比喻绝佳,同时写出了花之凋败与人之愁苦。

32. "intoxicated in Flowers Shade" (Light mists, dense clouds, and a long day in melancholy) by Li Qingzhao

Light mists, dense clouds, and a long day in melancholy. The incense is burning in the golden beast censer. Again, it is the Double Ninth Festival. Through jade pillows and silk screens, the coolness begins to penetrate in the middle of the night.

After drinking wine by the eastern hedge at dusk, subtle fragrance perfumes the sleeves. Do not say this is not doleful. Western wind rolls the curtain up, and I am more emaciated than the yellow flowers.

【 Commentary 】

During the Double Ninth Festival, the poet is drinking wine and appreciating chrysanthemums. Yet she still could not expel her inner sorrows. In the last three lines, a gloomy mood is created by the scene that the western wind stirs the curtain, and the poet likens herself to the yellow flowers. The character "emaciated" is an excellent word choice, for it is appropriate not only for the fading flowers, but for the sorrowful person as well.

南詞新譜

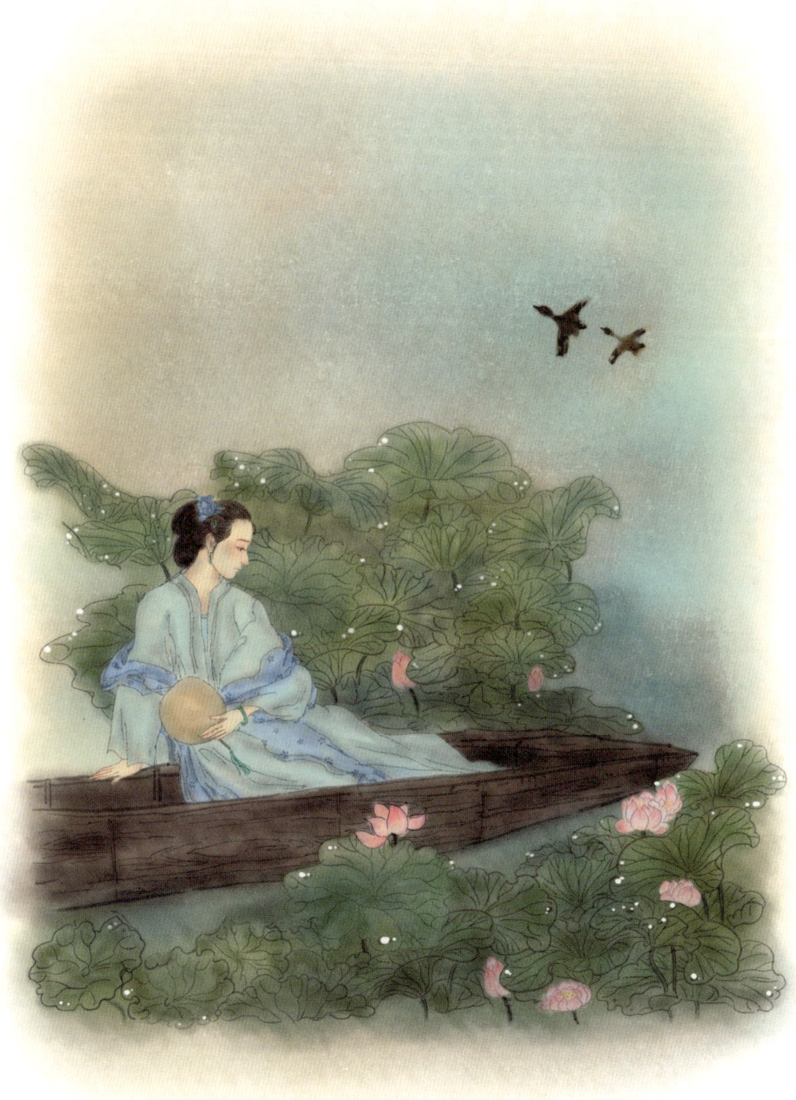

33. 李清照《如梦令·常记溪亭日暮》

【原文】

　　常记溪亭日暮,沉醉不知归路。兴尽晚回舟,误入藕花深处。争渡,争渡。惊起一滩鸥鹭。

【释文】

　　记得曾经在溪边的亭子中游赏,直到天色已暮,喝得大醉的我一时不知道回家的路。直到酒兴过去,小船慢慢趁夜返回,才发现不小心划进了荷花深密之处。想要夺路前进,拼命划呀划,却惊动了栖息在沙滩上的水鸟,扑棱棱振翅飞起。

【解析】

　　这首词乃词人早期的作品,记述了一次郊游:词人因游赏晚归,又因醉酒而走错了路,最后由于夺路前进将沙滩上的鸥鸟惊飞。全词运用白描的手法,写得生动而富有情趣,同时也刻画了主人公潇洒天真的形象。

33. "A Dream-like Song" (I often recall the dusk at the pavilion by a stream)
by Li Qingzhao

I often recall the dusk at the pavilion by a stream. Completely drunk, I do not know the way back. When all pleasure was spent, I returned on a boat at night, but strayed deep into lotus flowers. Struggled to get through, struggled to get through! It startled a beach of gulls and herons.

【 Commentary 】

This early work by Li Qingzhao describes her returning from an outing. It is late and the poet is totally drunk, so she takes the wrong way. When she struggles through the lotus flowers, the gulls and herons on the beach are all startled. The lyric is full of life and fun. Its plain language outlines an image of a poet who is native and unrestrained.

南詞敘錄

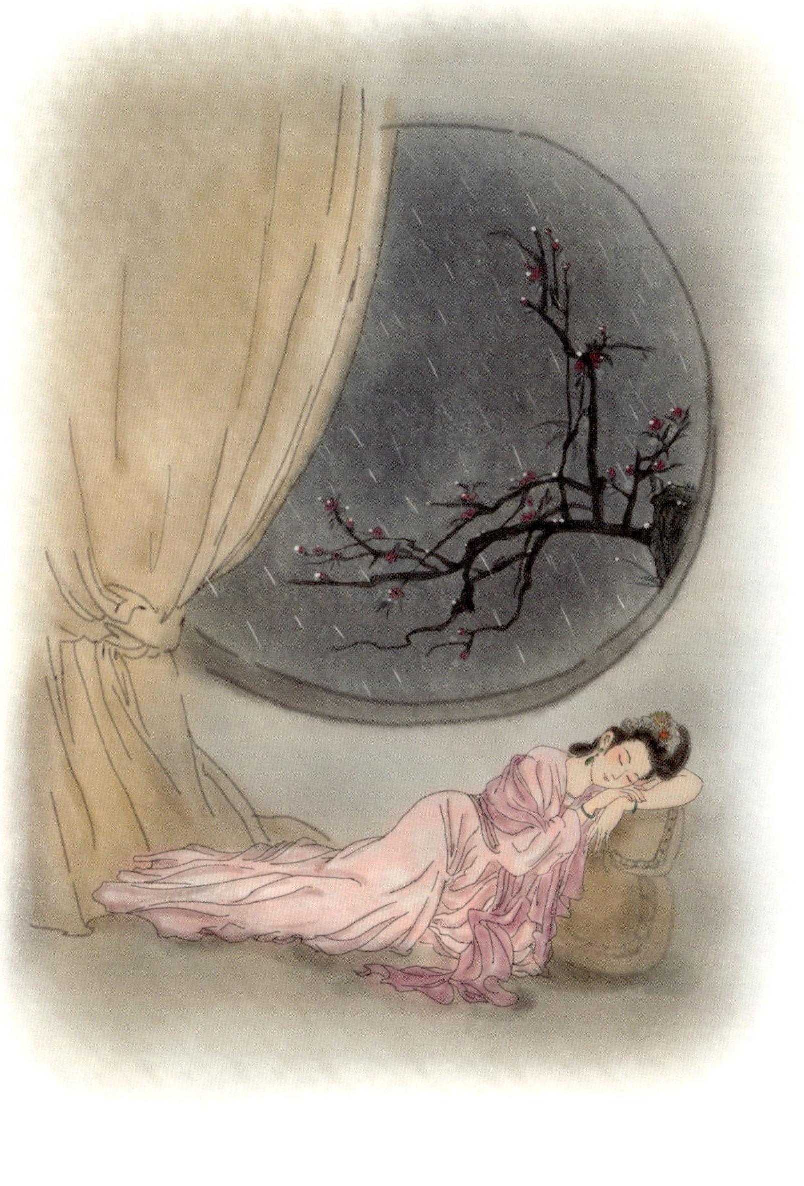

34. 李清照《如梦令·昨夜雨疏风骤》

【原文】

　　昨夜雨疏风骤,浓睡不消残酒。试问卷帘人,却道海棠依旧。知否,知否?应是绿肥红瘦。

【释文】

　　昨天夜里雨小风急,我虽睡得酣畅,然而因喝酒留下的残余的醉意却并未完全消除。于是问那正在卷帘的侍女,回答说,海棠花还和从前一样。知道吗?知道吗?应该是绿叶更加繁茂,而红花日渐凋零了。

【解析】

　　这首词是词人早期的作品,反映的是词人悠闲、风雅的生活情调。结尾"绿肥红瘦",将花和叶子拟人化,用语形象、生动。

34. "A Dreamy Chant" (Last night, the rain was light and the wind was rapid)
by Li Qingzhao

Last night, the rain was light and the wind was rapid. Deep sleep did not dispel the residual wine. I ask the curtain raiser, she answers, "The cherry apple flowers are still the same." Know it, or not? Know it, or not? It should be that the green is fat and the red is thin.

【 Commentary 】

This is an early work of the poet. The whole lyric reflects the poet's relaxed attitude and elegant taste in life. The last line personifies the flowers and leaves, and its language is vivid and impressive.

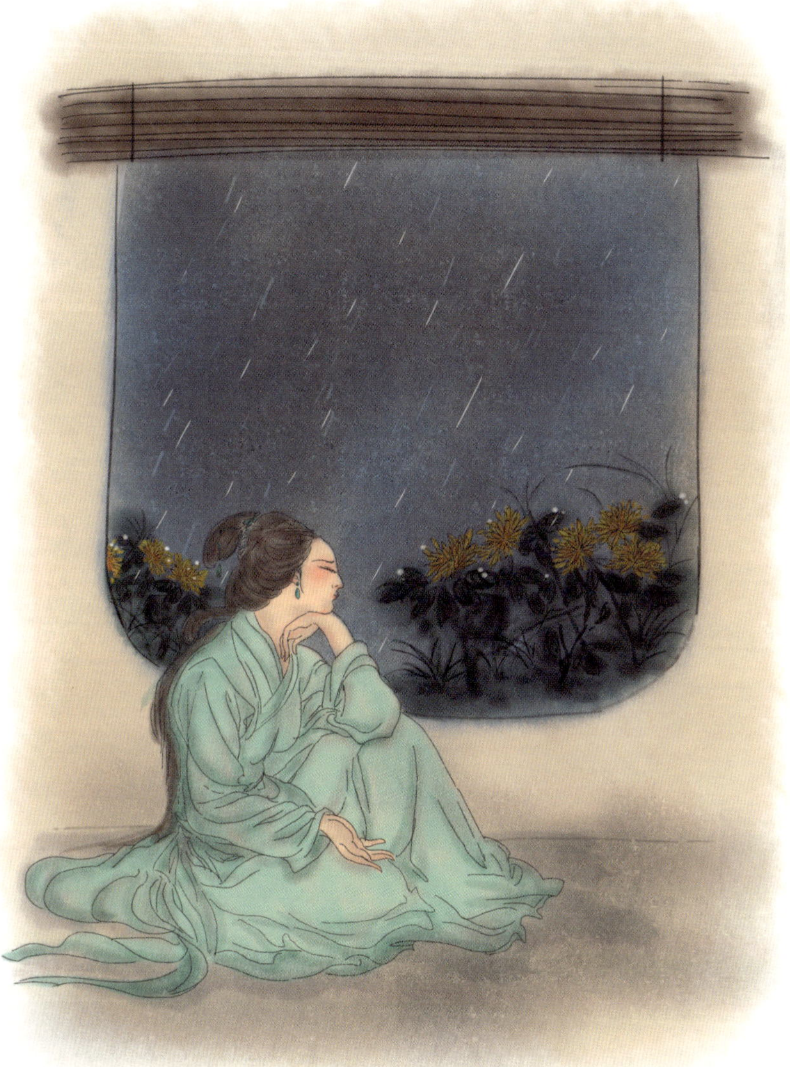

35. 李清照《声声慢·寻寻觅觅》

【原文】

　　寻寻觅觅，冷冷清清，凄凄惨惨戚戚。乍暖还寒时候，最难将息。三杯两盏淡酒，怎敌他、晚来风急！雁过也，正伤心，却是旧时相识。

　　满地黄花堆积，憔悴损，如今有谁堪摘？守着窗儿，独自怎生得黑！梧桐更兼细雨，到黄昏、点点滴滴。这次第，怎一个愁字了得！

【释文】

　　我若有所失地四处寻找，然而却一无所获。只有一片冷落凄清的场景，加重了我内心的惨淡悲戚。这样忽冷忽暖、变化无常的季节，最难调养好身体。仅靠几杯薄酒，怎么能抵御傍晚时分急骤的西风？大雁飞过，正让我伤心（无信可寄），却发现正是以前替我传信的老朋友。

　　一丛丛的菊花遍开，像是堆积在地面上，然而花儿已憔悴，现在还有什么可摘的呢？我独自一人守在窗口，对此情景，怎样挨到天黑？梧桐叶落伴着蒙蒙细雨，到黄昏时，一点点、一滴滴地飘下来。这样的情形，一个"愁"字怎能概括！

35. "Adagio of Resonance" (Seeking and searching) by Li Qingzhao

Seeking and searching; lonely and lonesome; desolate, dismal and depressed. While it is getting warmer, the cold still lingers. It is most difficult to rest. Three or two cups of thin wine, how could they hold off the swift wind at night? As wild geese fly by, I am heart-broken. But they are the old acquaintances of mine.

On the ground, yellow flowers piled up. So grief-worn. Who would pick them now? Staying by the window, how could I alone pass the time till it is dark? Drizzle is falling on wutong trees, at dusk, drop by drop, drip by drip. At a time like this, how could a single word "sorrow" sufficiently spell everything?

【解析】

　　这首词当是词人晚期的作品。整首词通过一系列深秋之景,如大雁、菊花、梧桐、细雨等,来表达内心孤独凄冷的愁绪。开头三句,连用十四个叠字,自然妥帖,将其怅然若失的感受及周遭环境的凄冷对她造成的影响写得十分细腻。而结尾"梧桐更兼细雨,到黄昏、点点滴滴"三句,则既富有音乐性,又更强调了前文环境的凄冷。

【 Commentary 】

This is one of the late works by the poet Li Qingzhao. Through vivid depiction of a series of images typically seen in late autumn, such as wild geese, chrysanthemums, wutong trees, and drizzles, etc., the poet conveys her inner sorrows and feelings of desolation. The repetition of the characters in the first three lines is natural and appropriate. It accurately conveys the delicate feelings of depression and loss brought by the doleful surroundings. The lines in the second stanza that "drizzle is falling on wutong trees, at dusk, drop by drop, drip by drip" are musical verses which highlight the desolation of the environment.

酒肆

36. 朱敦儒《鹧鸪天·我是清都山水郎》
西都作

【原文】

我是清都山水郎,天教分付与疏狂。曾批给雨支风券,累上留云借月章。

诗万首,酒千觞。几曾著眼看侯王。玉楼金阙慵归去,且插梅花醉洛阳。

【释文】

我是天宫中管理山水的郎官,生性疏懒、狂放不拘。曾经奉旨批过支配风雨的手令,也多次上奏过留住云彩、借走月亮。

我曾赋诗万首,醉酒千杯。何时将王侯将相放在眼里。即便是去华丽的天宫做官我也不愿,只想插一枝梅花,醉倒在洛阳城中。

【解析】

此词题作"西都作",即作于洛阳。词的上片写自己爱好山水、放荡不羁的天性。"曾批"两句设想自己管理风、雨、云、月的细节,充满了浪漫的精神。下片则进一步写自己淡泊名利、纵情山水。全词自然流畅,是一首脍炙人口的佳作。

36. "Partridge Sky" (I am the officer of mountain and river in clear capital)
by Zhu Dunru
Written at Western Capital

I am the officer of mountain and river in clear capital. The heaven grants me unrestrained character and unbounded enthusiasm. I have approved the edicts of rain and wind. For many times, I submitted memorials to retain clouds and borrow the moon.

Ten thousands of poems; one thousand cups of wine. I never lay my eyes on Marquises and Kings. Even for jade tower and gold terrace, I am reluctant to return. I will just insert mume flowers and get drunk in Luoyang.

【Commentary】

The title of this lyric is "Written at Western Capital," and the Western Capital refers to Luoyang. The first stanza shows that the poet loves nature and is free of any restraints. The poet imagines in the second couplet that he is in charge of the wind, the rain, the clouds and the moon. The details are filled with romantic elements. The second stanza further reveals the poet is indifferent to fame and wealth, and dedicates himself to nature. The flow of the verse is smooth and natural. The lyric is a very popular piece of good writing.

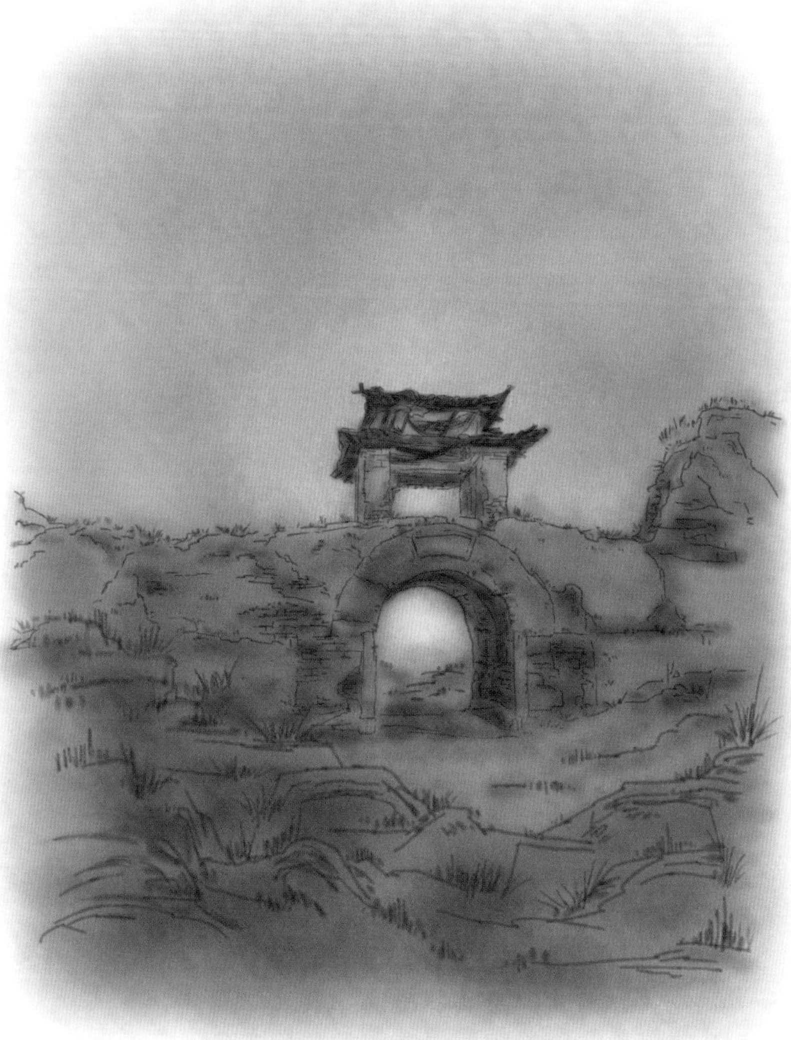

37. 张元幹《贺新郎·梦绕神州路》
送胡邦衡待制赴新州

【原文】

梦绕神州路。怅秋风,连营画角,故宫离黍。底事昆仑倾砥柱,九地黄流乱注。聚万落、千村狐兔。天意从来高难问,况人情老易悲难诉!更南浦,送君去。

凉生岸柳催残暑。耿斜河,疏星淡月,断云微度。万里江山知何处?回首对床夜语。雁不到、书成谁与?目尽青天怀今古,肯儿曹恩怨相尔汝?举大白,听《金缕》。

【释文】

梦魂还一直牵绕着中原故土。而今秋风起,虽然军营之中,号角阵阵,沦陷的汴京等地,已然禾黍深深,一片衰败。为什么昆仑山这根天柱也会倒塌,而使得遍地黄河水乱流、泛滥成灾,无数的村落狐兔成群呢。天意向来高高在上,难以预测,况且人们越老越容易悲伤,这悲伤难以诉说!而在这南浦之地,我竟然又要送你远去。

暑日将近,凉意顿生,你我在这杨柳岸边道别。天上明亮的银河移转,朵朵微云缓缓地飘过去。而后江山阻隔,相距万里,哪能知道你在什么地方呢?回想过去你我亲密无间,深夜对谈。而今你

37. "Congratulations to the Groom" (In dreams, I wander around the paths of the Divine Land) by Zhang Yuangan
Seeing Hu Bangheng off for Xinzhou

In dreams, I wander around the paths of the Divine Land. Disappointed autumn wind; blows of patterned horns from tent to tent, the old palaces are desolate. How could the pillar of Kunlun Mountain fall down, and the water of the Yellow River flows chaotically everywhere, and foxes and hares are gathering in thousands of tribes and villages. The intention of the heaven is always too profound to be known. In addition, when people are getting old, it is easy to be sorrowful, but hard to share feelings. I am seeing you off, at the southern riverside.

Coldness grows from the riverside willows chases away the remnant summer heat. Bright slanting river; sparse stars and pale moon; broken clouds slowly drift. Where to find the rivers and mountains stretching out of view? I remember the night talk with you sitting in bed. Geese will not go to the place you are heading toward, so who will pass the letters I write? I look into the blue sky till the very end of it, and think of the past and the present. How could we behave like young men and have personal feelings? Hold up a wine cup and listen to the song of *Golden Threads*.

去了这大雁都到不了的地方，我的书信写好，谁能代为传递呢？放眼远望，由古到今想到多少事情，哪能像孩子似的专讲那些个人恩怨呢？还是让我们举起酒杯，来听一曲《金缕》吧。

【解析】

　　此词乃胡铨因上书反对宋金议和，被谪新州（今广东新兴），途经福州时，张元幹为其送行所作。整首词表现了词人对于山河沦落的悲痛，对投降派的愤怒，以及对胡铨的同情。慷慨悲凉，有磊落之气。

【 Commentary 】

The poet wrote this lyric when he met his friend Hu Bangheng. Hu submitted a letter to the emperor to oppose the negotiation of a peace agreement between the Southern Song and the Jin, hence, he was demoted from his position and sent to Xinzhou in the South. On his way, Hu met Zhang at Fuzhou. The whole song expresses the poet's sorrow for the downfall of his country, hatred to those who support surrender, and sympathy for his friend Hu. It presents the readers with a sense of passion, desolation and uprightness.

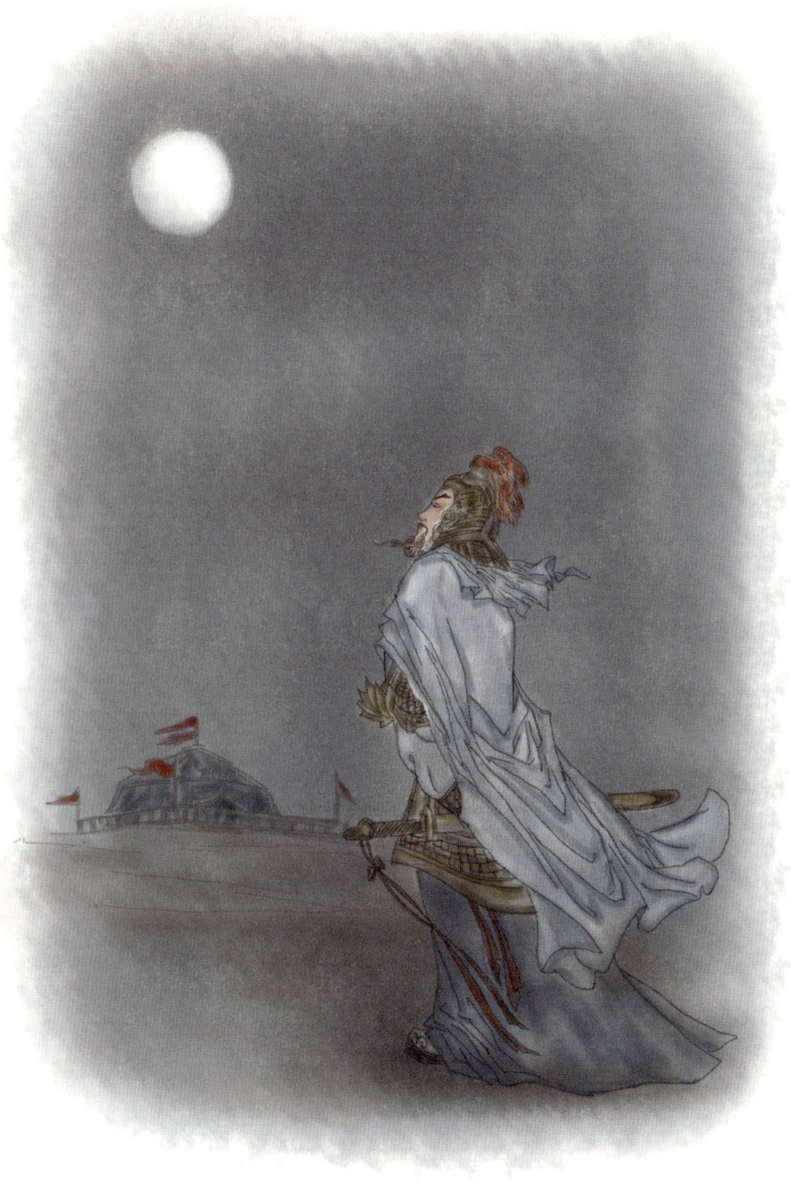

38. 岳飞《小重山·昨夜寒蛩不住鸣》

【原文】

　　昨夜寒蛩不住鸣。惊回千里梦,已三更。起来独自绕阶行。人悄悄,帘外月胧明。

　　白首为功名。旧山松竹老,阻归程。欲将心事付瑶琴。知音少,弦断有谁听?

【释文】

　　寒秋已至,昨夜的蟋蟀不停地哀鸣。向千里之外的故乡挺进的好梦就这样被惊醒,时过三更。起床独自绕着台阶,来回踱步。四周静悄悄的,帘外月光微明。

　　长存为国建功立业之心,直到生出白发。故乡的松竹渐老,然而归家的路程依然被阻隔。想要将满腹的心事付与瑶琴。可叹知音稀少,即使将琴弦弹断,又有谁会来听?

【解析】

　　绍兴八年(1138年),南宋与金议和,岳飞等主战派因建议不被采纳而深为苦闷,这首词似应作于此时。词的上片着重写景,词人梦回故园,醒来之后惆怅不已,只得月下徘徊。下片着重抒情,多年在外征战,然而功业难成。最后三句更是反映了知音难遇、有志难伸的痛苦。

38. "Manifold Little Hill" (Last night the autumn crickets chirped incessantly)
by Yue Fei

Last night the autumn crickets chirped incessantly, and startled my dream in which I returned home a thousand miles away. It was already the third watch. I got up and strolled around the stairs alone. There was no other human, and the moon shone bright over the curtains.

The white hairs are for the merits and fame. In old mountains, pines and bamboos become aged. A returning journey is impeded. I desire to confide my heart to the jade zither. Soul-mate listeners are few, and who would hear it even if I break the strings?

【 Commentary 】

In 1138, the leaders of the Southern Song government and the Jin government were negotiating a peace agreement. Yue Fei and his supporters felt extremely depressed because their suggestions of fighting against the Jin soldiers were not considered by the rulers. The lyric was probably written during this historical period. The first stanza mainly writes about the scenery. The poet dreams of returning to his hometown and feels depressed after waking up. He could do nothing but wander around underneath the moon. The poet expresses his emotions in the second stanza: the war lasts for years, but he still achieves nothing. The last three lines display the poet's grief, for it is so hard to fulfill his goals and find a bosom friend.

南詞敘錄

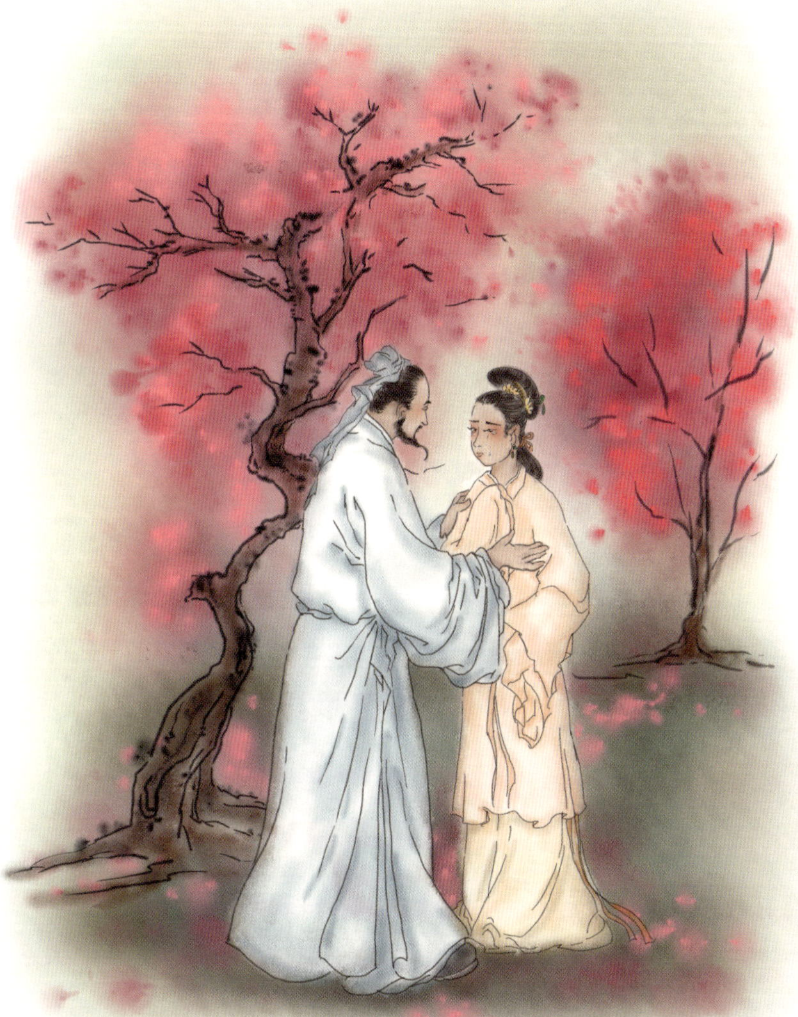

39. 陆游《钗头凤·红酥手》

【原文】

　　红酥手,黄縢酒,满城春色宫墙柳。东风恶,欢情薄,一怀愁绪,几年离索。错,错,错!

　　春如旧,人空瘦,泪痕红浥鲛绡透。桃花落,闲池阁,山盟虽在,锦书难托。莫,莫,莫!

【释文】

　　你红润而白嫩的手,捧着盛有黄縢酒(黄封酒,宋时官酒以黄纸封口,故而得名)的杯子殷勤劝酒的场景犹在,如今虽春色满城,而你却已如宫墙中的柳树,可望而不可即。东风实在可恶,将欢聚的浓情渐渐吹薄,只剩下了满怀的愁怨以及几年来离群索居的生活。哎,这一切都是错啊!

　　眼前之景正如从前那样的春日,但你却白白地消瘦了,思及往日,沾着胭脂的泪水湿透了手帕。而桃花已谢,池台楼阁也被冷落,虽然誓言仍在,却再难以互通书信。哎,罢了罢了!

39. "Phoenix Hairpin" (Pink tender hands)
by Lu You

Pink tender hands; yellow-sealed wine; a town full of spring colors, and willows within palaces walls. Eastern wind is unrelenting; happy times are rare; one cup of sorrowful feelings; several years of separation and desolation. Wrong, wrong, wrong!

Spring is as the same; you become emaciated in vain; rouged tears soak the silk handkerchief. Peach flowers fall; ponds and pavilions are lonesome; though the mountain-firm oath is there, brocade letters are hard to be sent. No! No! No!

【解析】

　　据《齐东野语》等书记载,这首词描写了词人陆游与其妻唐婉的爱情悲剧。陆游与唐婉婚后感情和谐,却因男方母亲的反对被迫分离。后来两人各自重新组建家庭,这首词描写的是词人在一次春游过程中与唐氏的相遇。整首词表现了两人之间的相思之切以及对阻碍他们的势力的怨恨,感情的凄楚和无可奈何跃然纸上。

【 Commentary 】

　　The tragic love story of the poet and his wife Tang Wan (?) has been recorded in many books, such as *Hearsays from Qidong*. After marrying Tang, Lu You led a happy and harmonious family life. But his mother strongly opposed their marriage, so they had to divorce each other and form new families. This song writes about their encounter during a spring outing. It reflects their mutual affection and hatred toward the obstacles to their happy marriage. The feelings of sorrows and helplessness are vividly conveyed in the verses.

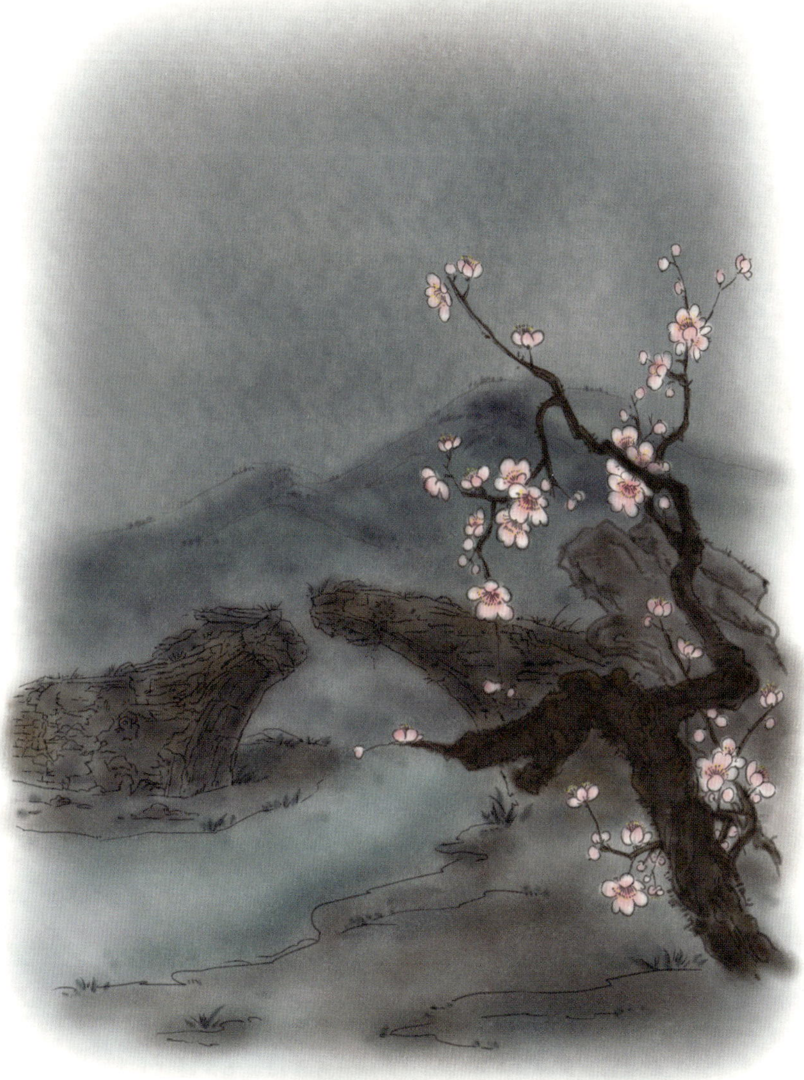

40. 陆游《卜算子·驿外断桥边》咏梅

【原文】

驿外断桥边,寂寞开无主。已是黄昏独自愁,更著风和雨。
无意苦争春,一任群芳妒。零落成泥碾作尘,只有香如故。

【释文】

驿站外的断桥边,梅花寂寞地开放,无人过问。已到黄昏时分,它本已独自愁苦,却又遭受风雨的摧残。

它无意与百花争奇斗艳,抢占春光,也任由它们妒忌。即使它凋零之后,化成了泥土,碾压成了灰尘,散发出来的香气还和以前一样。

【解析】

这是一首吟咏梅花的词。词的上片写梅花生长环境的恶劣,下片写梅花志趣和品格的高尚。通过对梅花不畏艰难、傲然绽放的描写,表现自己的志向和操守。

40. "Divination" (Outside the post house, and beside the broken bridge.) by Lu You
Ode to Mume Flowers

Outside the post house, and beside the broken bridge, they bloom in loneliness and obscurity. It is already dusk, and they are in melancholy all alone, and suffering from wind and rain.

With no intention of craving spring for themselves alone, they are envied by various flowers. The fallen flowers turn into mud or are ground into dust, but their fragrances will be the same.

【 Commentary 】

This is an ode to mume flowers. The first half describes the severe natural environment in which mume flowers grow, and the second half highlights the noble character of the flowers. Fearless of the difficulties, mume flowers proudly blossom of themselves. The poet aims to declare his aspiration and integrity through his description of the flowers in this lyric.

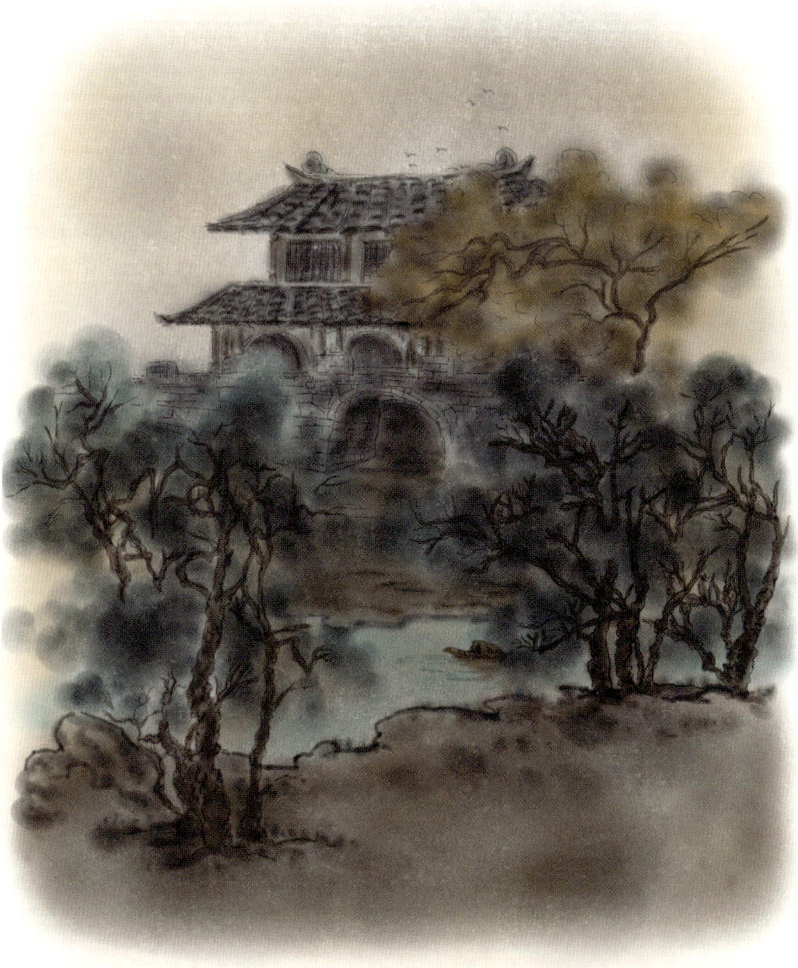

41. 张孝祥《六州歌头·长淮望断》

【原文】

　　长淮望断,关塞莽然平。征尘暗,霜风劲,悄边声。黯销凝！追想当年事,殆天数,非人力。洙泗上,弦歌地,亦膻腥。隔水毡乡,落日牛羊下,区脱纵横。看名王宵猎,骑火一川明,笳鼓悲鸣,遣人惊。

　　念腰间箭,匣中剑,空埃蠹,竟何成！时易失,心徒壮,岁将零,渺神京。干羽方怀远,静烽燧,且休兵。冠盖使,纷驰骛,若为情！闻道中原遗老,常南望、翠葆霓旌。使行人到此,忠愤气填膺,有泪如倾。

【释文】

　　极目远望淮河,关塞隐没在一片茂盛的草木丛中。道上的征尘已经暗淡,北风正在劲吹,边境却寂然无声。身临此情此境,只能默默神伤。回想当年中原失守,大概是天意如此,不是人力所能挽回的。而今,连孔子曾经讲学的洙水、泗水畔,礼乐兴盛之地,也遭金兵践踏。只一水之隔,便是搭满了毡房的金兵聚集地,黄昏日落,牛羊成群回栏,金兵的哨所纵横遍地。而看那金兵夜间仍在狩猎,兵士们手执的火把将整个淮河照得通明。胡笳声声,鼓角悲鸣,

41. "Preludes to the Songs of Six States" (I look at the long Huai River in distance until it vanishes) by Zhang Xiaoxiang

I look at the long Huai River in distance until it vanishes. The border fortresses are as high as the overgrown weeds. Battle dust becomes dim; frosty wind is strong; sounds of the borders are hushed. I am dispirited and depressed! In reminiscence, the affair of that year had been destined, and human efforts cannot battle with celestial powers. The area along the Zhu and Si Rivers, used to be a land of string music, now reeks of blood smells. Across the water, hair tents occupy our homeland; under the setting sun, cattle and sheep are coming home; guard posts are all over this land. The chieftains are hunting at night, cavalry's torches form a bright flow; tartar pipes and drums resonate sorrowfully, which give people a fright.

I think of the arrows by waist, and the sword in cask. In vain they are stained with dust and bugs, what a waste! Time is easily lost; the great aspiration is still there; another year is about to lapse; distant is the divine capital. Musical instruments are used to appease those in distance. Beacon fires will be put out, and a truce will be called. Ambassadors hurry to and fro, and how shameful! I heard that the people of the central plains often look southward, wishing for the imperial ensigns and colorful pennants. It made people who have come here feel indignant, and pour out their tears.

使人胆寒心惊。

　　思及那腰间的羽箭和匣中的宝剑，怕是已经空遭尘封和虫蛀，而满怀壮志，又做成了什么事呢！时机容易失去，即使有壮烈的胸怀，眼看一年将尽，都城汴京依然渺远不可到。而统治者也借口以礼乐安抚少数民族，使其归顺，已经放弃了抵抗，边境戒备松弛，已经见不到烽烟，双方暂时休兵。求和的使者，往来奔驰，怎么也不觉得难为情呢？听说留在中原地区的父老，常常向南远望，盼望大宋皇帝的车驾能够回来。此情此景，都使过路的行人身临此地，忠义愤慨之气填满胸膛，热泪如雨般止不住倾流。

【解析】

　　此词上片写淮河对岸沦为金人占领区的景象，下片写词人空有一腔报国热情，然而世易时移，功业难成。朝廷又一味求和，使得中原沦陷区的百姓只能一次次失望。义愤悲痛之情交加，整首词表达淋漓痛快，读起来令人拍案叫绝。

【 Commentary 】

　　The first stanza writes about the scene of Huai river where the Jin soldiers has already occupied. The second stanza shows that the poet is an enthusiastic patriot, but it is difficult to achieve military merits since things change with the time. The rulers are seeking to reach a peace agreement and the commoners in the central plain occupied by enemies feel extremely desperate. In this song, indignation, sorrows and bitterness all mix together. The lyric is written in a straightforward manner and is an amazing piece of verse.

南詞敘錄

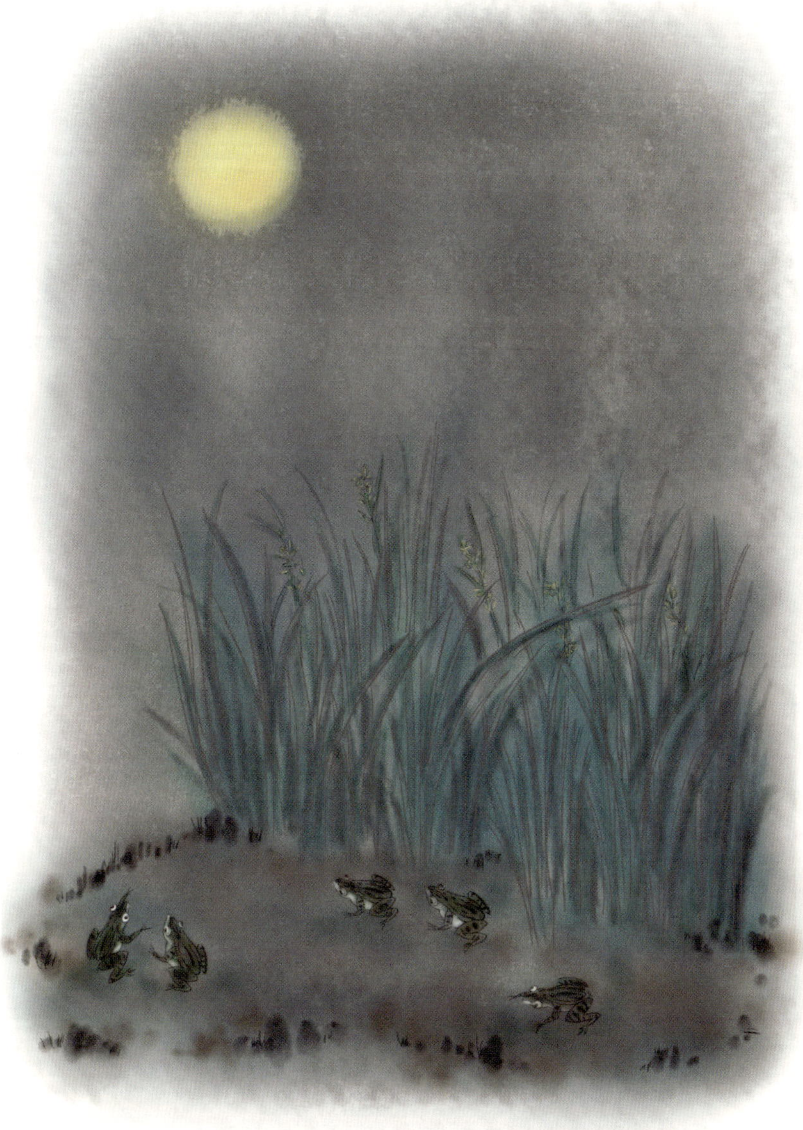

42. 辛弃疾《西江月·明月别枝惊鹊》
夜行黄沙道中

【原文】

明月别枝惊鹊,清风半夜鸣蝉。稻花香里说丰年,听取蛙声一片。

七八个星天外,两三点雨山前。旧时茅店社林边,路转溪桥忽见。

【释文】

明月升起,惊醒了栖息在枝头的喜鹊;清风拂过,深夜的蝉鸣越发清晰。在稻谷的香气里,人们边谈论着丰收的年景,边听着阵阵蛙声。

远处的天边稀稀落落地挂着几颗星星,山前淅淅沥沥的小雨降落。从溪边的小桥转个弯,土地庙树丛旁那家旧时见过的茅店又出现在眼前。

【解析】

这是一首描写夏夜乡村风物之作,语言浅白流畅,描写生动。对于丰年的展望和美好的自然之景,使作者处于一种难得的身心愉悦之中。而结尾处"旧时茅店"的突然出现,也体现了词人由于沉浸在周围的美景中而入迷的情态。用语朴素,足见词人功力的深厚。

42. "Western River Moon" (A bright moon over yonder branches startles the magpies)
by Xin Qiji
A Night Trip on Yellow Sand Road

A bright moon over yonder branches startles the magpies. A clear wind at midnight makes the cicadas chirp. Amid the aroma of rice flowers, a talk of a harvest year. Hear the croak of the frogs here and there. Seven or eight stars in the faraway sky; two or three drops of rain before the hills. The old straw store by the side of the communal woods, is suddenly seen when the road turns at the stream bridge.

【Commentary】

This lyric describes a summer night village scene. Its language is simple, plain and vivid. The expectation for a harvest year and the beauty of the natural scenery bring a visual and emotional joy to the poet. In the end, the sudden appearance of the "old straw store" indicates that the poet is totally absorbed in the beautiful scenery. The poet's superb skills lie in his use of simple and plain language.

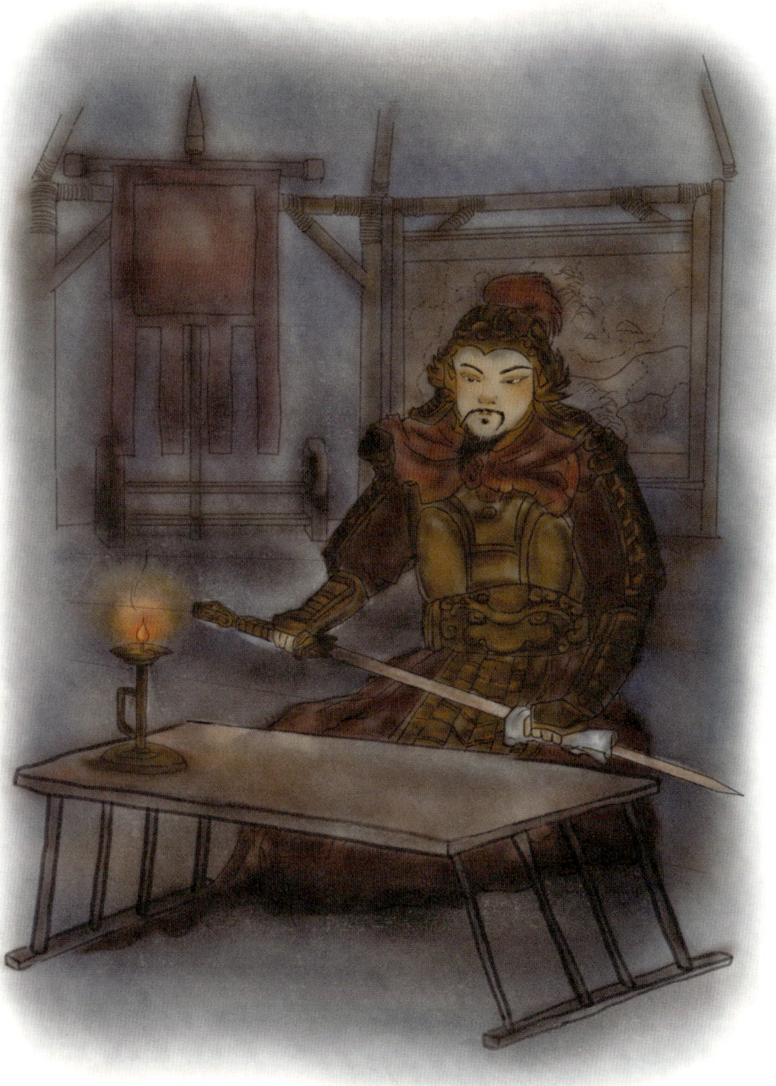

43. 辛弃疾《破阵子·醉里挑灯看剑》
为陈同甫赋壮语以寄之

【原文】

　　醉里挑灯看剑,梦回吹角连营。八百里分麾下炙,五十弦翻塞外声,沙场秋点兵。

　　马作的卢飞快,弓如霹雳弦惊。了却君王天下事,赢得生前身后名,可怜白发生!

【释文】

　　醉后拨亮油灯观看宝剑,梦中号角声响彻军营。各营的士兵都分到了烤熟的牛肉,各式的乐器奏出了雄壮的歌曲,正是战场秋日检阅军队之时。

　　战马奔驰如的卢马一样迅疾,箭离弦时弓弦如惊雷般乍响。帮助君王完成收复中原、平定天下的大事,博得生前和死后的荣名。哎,可怜一梦醒来,惊觉白发已生。

【解析】

　　收复河山的事业未竟,个人的功名未成,只能任凭白发陡生,而横戈跃马、杀敌立功的壮烈事迹只能出现在梦中。整首词流露出浓烈的壮志难酬的悲愤。

43. "Breaking the Formation" (In drunkenness, I trim the lamp wick to see the sword)
by Xin Qiji
Encouragement Sent to Chen Tongfu

In drunkenness, I trim the lamp wick to see the sword. In dream, horns are blown from tent to tent. Soldiers share grilled beef under flags. Fifty string instruments play sounds of borders. It is an autumn military parade in the field.

The horses run fast as if they were flying. The bows release the arrows like thundering. Fulfill the mission under heaven for the kings, and win the fame during and after my lifetime. What a pity! White hair grows!

【 Commentary 】

The whole lyric displays a strong sense of grief of unfulfillment. The poet is still not able to recapture the lost territory and achieve military merits, but his white hair grows more and more. The heroic deeds of riding the horse and killing the enemies could only appear in his dream.

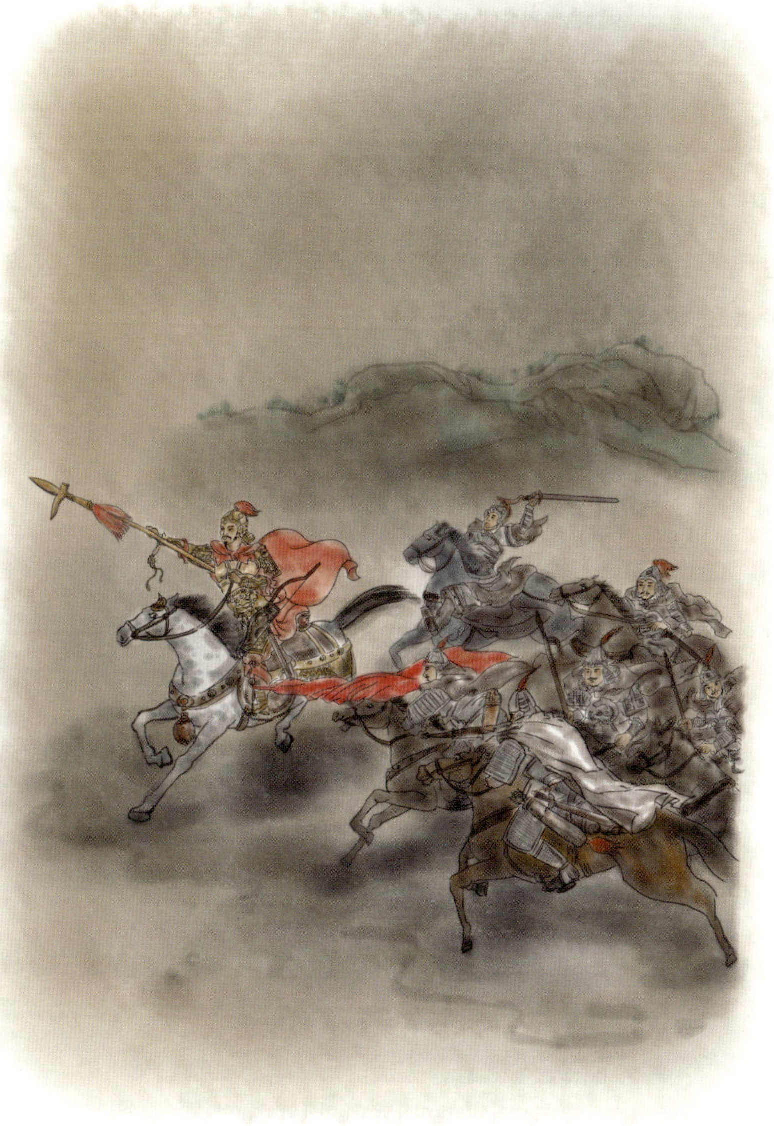

44. 辛弃疾《永遇乐·千古江山》
京口北固亭怀古

【原文】

　　千古江山，英雄无觅，孙仲谋处。舞榭歌台，风流总被，雨打风吹去。斜阳草树，寻常巷陌，人道寄奴曾住。想当年、金戈铁马，气吞万里如虎。

　　元嘉草草，封狼居胥，赢得仓皇北顾。四十三年，望中犹记，烽火扬州路。可堪回首，佛狸祠下，一片神鸦社鼓！凭谁问、廉颇老矣，尚能饭否？

【释文】

　　千百年来的江山仍在，而像孙仲谋那样的英雄人物，再也无处寻找了。六朝的歌舞楼台，风流事迹，早已被雨打风吹，消逝无痕。而当夕阳斜照在树木与草丛之上，人们说道那平常的街巷也曾是宋武帝刘裕居住的地方。怀想当年，他曾带领强健的兵马北征，气吞山河，如虎般勇猛。

　　然而到了宋文帝刘义隆时，由于草率出兵，妄图封狼居胥山而还，结果落得大败而归，仓皇南逃。如今我奉命南渡已有四十三年了，然而登亭眺望，当年扬州一带的抗金烽火，依然清晰地记得。怎能忍受，这被敌兵侵略过的地方，如今鼓声阵阵，一片热闹的祭

44. "Forever in Happiness" (Among rivers and mountains since the ancient times) by Xin Qiji
Thoughts on the Past at Beigu Pavilion in Capital Entrance

Among rivers and mountains since the ancient times, heroes such as Sun Zhongmou are nowhere to find. The waterside dancing halls and singing podiums are there, but gallant deeds are already swept away by winds and rain. The slanting sun, grass and trees; ordinary alleys and paths; people say Liu Yu once lived here. Think of those years; with metal halberds and armored horses, he charged like a tiger, swallowing up ten thousand miles.

His son waged a battle in Yuanjia in haste, but they were defeated at Langjuxu Mountains, resulting in a panic northern expedition. Forty-three years passed, and gazing at the central plains, I still remember how beacon fires blazed the way to Yangzhou. How can I bear to see that sacred crows among the holy drums in the Bili Temple? Who would still care to ask: Lian Po is old, is he alright to have his meal?

祀景象。还有谁会来问我这个已经年老的"廉颇"（战国时期赵国名将），如今饭量怎样，是否还能打仗？

【解析】

  这首词乃辛弃疾六十多岁高龄，任镇江知府时所作。整首词通过怀古，表达出词人对抗金行动的支持，但同时反对草草行事，希望通过充足的准备来赢得抗金战事的胜利。整首词风格沉郁悲凉，虽用了很多的典故，但贴合文意，含义丰富，使得这首词成为稼轩词中的佳作。

【 Commentary 】

This lyric was written by Xin when he served as the magistrate of Zhenjiang prefecture over the age of sixty. His thoughts on the past actually declare a clear stance in supporting the anti-Jin activities. At the same time, he opposes to take actions in a brash way. A full preparation, in Xin's view, is prerequisite for the victory over the Jin soldiers. The whole lyric presents the readers a sense of gloom and desolation. The allusions are pertinent and rich in implications, and these, among other elements, contribute to the popularity of this masterpiece of Xin Qiji.

南詞敘錄

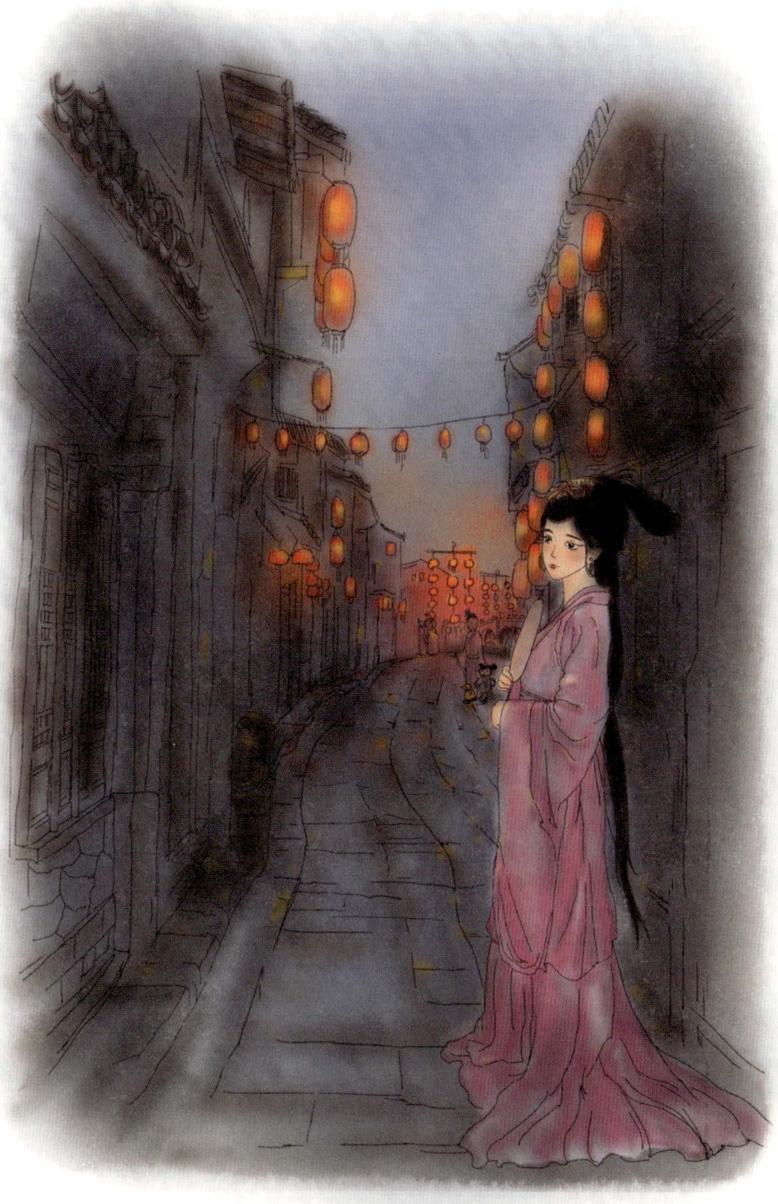

45. 辛弃疾《青玉案·东风夜放花千树》
元夕

【原文】

　　东风夜放花千树，更吹落、星如雨。宝马雕车香满路。凤箫声动，玉壶光转，一夜鱼龙舞。

　　蛾儿雪柳黄金缕，笑语盈盈暗香去。众里寻他千百度，蓦然回首，那人却在、灯火阑珊处。

【释文】

　　东风过处，花灯灿烂如千树花开，又似星星般飞舞。华丽的骏马和雕花的车辆往来行走，将香气洒满整条街道。箫声响起，明月渐落，鱼灯龙灯彻夜起舞。

　　佩戴着蛾儿、雪柳、黄金缕等饰物的姑娘们正说说笑笑地随人群走过，隐隐的香气散落。而我，在人群中寻找她千百次，也未找到。忽然回过头来，却见她正在那灯火稀落的地方。

【解析】

　　这首词是稼轩词中较为婉约绮丽的一首，词的上片写元宵节的热闹景象，下片写约会的场景。词人追慕这样一个不随众流、遗世独立的佳人，也表达了其自身不同于流俗和坚守节操的品质。

45. "Green Jade Table" (Eastern wind at night blows the flowers of a thousand trees open) by Xin Qiji
The First Night of New Year

Eastern wind at night blows the flowers of a thousand trees open, and blows adrift the sparks showering down like rain. Precious horses and carved carriages; fragrance fill up the road. Phoenix flutes music is played; the light of the jade flagon changes; a whole night of the dance of fish and dragons.

Moth-shaped hairpins, snow willows, and golden threads; among the laughter and chatter, the fragrance is fading away. In the crowds, I search for her countless times. Suddenly turning my head, I find her there, where the lights glow dimly.

【 Commentary 】

Among Xin's works, this lyric stands out for its taste of elegance and beautiful words. The first stanza focuses on the flourishing scene of the Lantern Festival, and the second stanza describes a rendezvous. The poet longs for such a fine, independent and unique lady who refuses to follow the crowd. And this also indicates the poet himself possesses similar integrities.

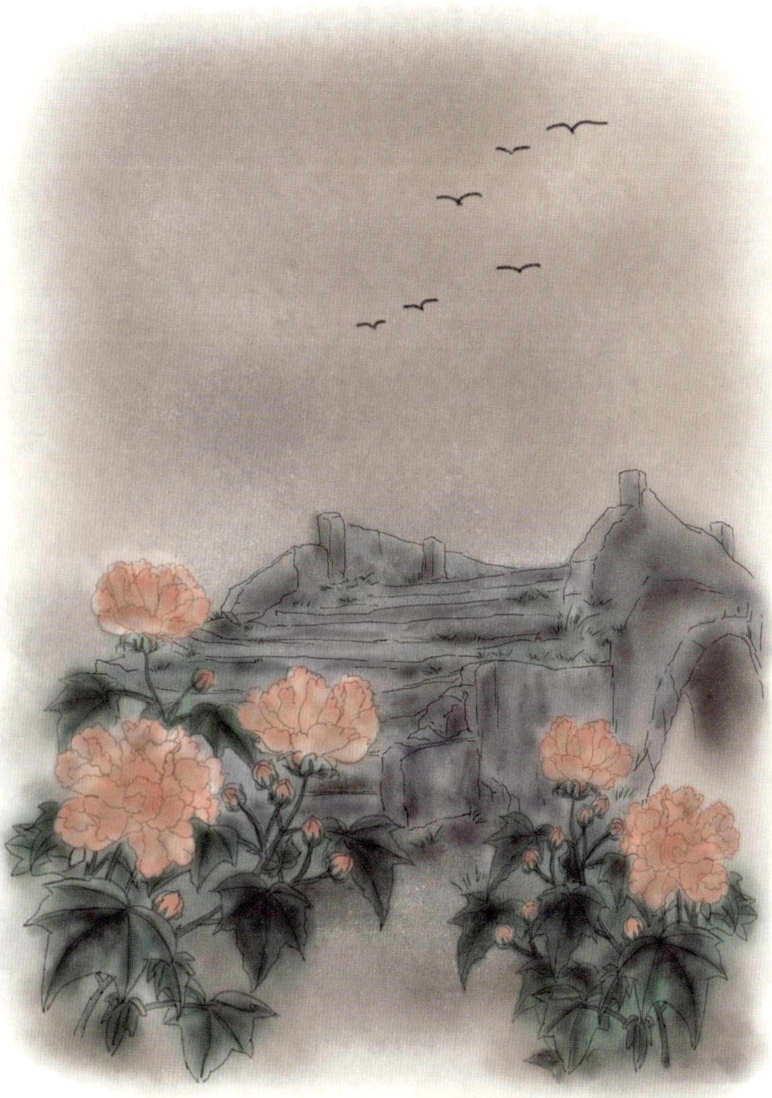

46. 姜夔《扬州慢·淮左名都》

【原文】

淳熙丙申至日,予过维扬。夜雪初霁,荠麦弥望。入其城,则四顾萧条,寒水自碧,暮色渐起,戍角悲吟。予怀怆然,感慨今昔,因自度此曲。千岩老人以为有"黍离"之悲也。

淮左名都,竹西佳处,解鞍少驻初程。过春风十里,尽荠麦青青。自胡马窥江去后,废池乔木,犹厌言兵。渐黄昏,清角吹寒,都在空城。

杜郎俊赏,算而今、重到须惊。纵豆蔻词工,青楼梦好,难赋深情。二十四桥仍在,波心荡、冷月无声。念桥边红药,年年知为谁生?

【释文】

我来到扬州这一淮南东路著名的都会,竹西亭一带风景秀丽的地方,解下马鞍,为我初次来此的旅程稍作停留。而原本春风十里的繁华都城,却尽是大片青青的荠菜麦苗。自从金兵向南侵犯过长江沿岸后,就连荒废的城池和大树都厌恶提到那场战争。渐渐到了黄昏,凄清的号角吹起,寒意布满整座空寂的城市。

扬州曾是诗人杜牧的游赏之地,料想如今他重游这里,也一定

46. "Yangzhou Adagio" (In this famed town, east of the Huai River) by Jiang Kui

In this famed town, east of the Huai River, and at the fine place called West of Bamboos, I take off the saddle to take a rest in the first leg of my journey. I passed ten miles in spring breeze, where nothing is seen except for the shepherd's purse and wheat so green. Since barbarian horses have crossed the river to trespass, abandoned ponds and mature trees remain, and to mention the word "war" is loathsome. Gradually, dusk arrives, the clear horns blow the coldness, echoing in the empty city.

Talented Du Mu loved this place, yet if he were here now, he would be confounded. Though skilled in composing verses describing young ladies or fine dreams in blue mansions, he would feel hard to express his deep feelings. The twenty-four bridges are still existent; ripples are gently undulating; the cold moon is silent. I think of the red peonies by the bridges, year after year, for whom do they bloom?

会感到惊讶。纵使他有写"豆蔻""青楼"诗的才华,也难再写出那样的深情了。二十四桥还在,水波荡漾,月亮倒映其中,寂静凄冷。而动乱之后,虽然桥边的芍药花仍然年年在春风中绽放,却不知道为谁而开了。

【解析】

这首词作于宋孝宗淳熙三年(1176年)冬至日,姜夔路过扬州,目睹了整座城市因金兵南侵造成的破坏。词以今昔强烈的对比,寄托了自己的哀思及对侵略者的愤恨,是姜夔少有的描写现实的佳作。

【 Commentary 】

This lyric was written on the Winter Solstice of 1176. Jiang Kui passed Yangzhou and saw that how the whole city was destroyed due to the invasion of Jin soldiers. The vivid contrast between the past the present in the lyric highlights the grief of the poet and his attitude of hatred toward the invaders. This is one of few Jiang's works that reflects the reality.

南詞新譜

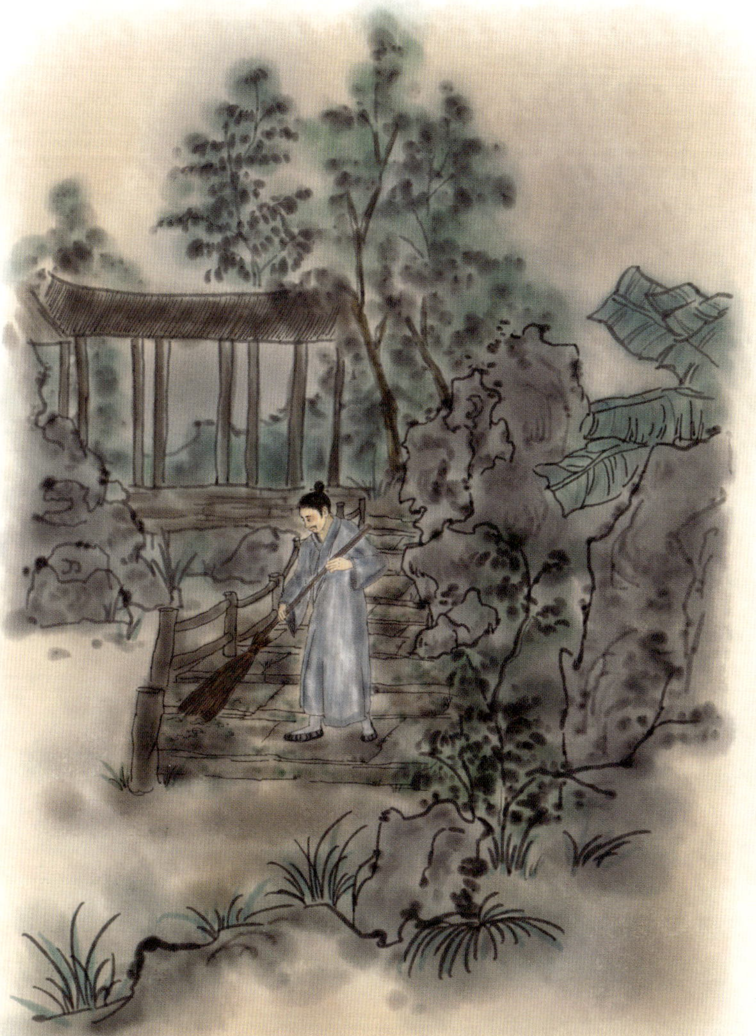

47. 吴文英《风入松·听风听雨过清明》

【原文】

　　听风听雨过清明，愁草《瘗花铭》。楼前绿暗分携路，一丝柳、一寸柔情。料峭春寒中酒，交加晓梦啼莺。

　　西园日日扫林亭，依旧赏新晴。黄蜂频扑秋千索，有当时、纤手香凝。惆怅双鸳不到，幽阶一夜苔生。

【释文】

　　在风雨交加的日子中，我度过了清明时节，满腔愁绪去起草《瘗花铭》之类的文字。楼前分别的路上，绿柳已经成荫。那一寸寸的柳丝正是我一寸寸的柔情。春日微寒之时，饮酒半酣，而纷乱的莺啼之声终将我从晓梦中惊醒。

　　我仍然天天都去西园，打扫那里的亭台园林，欣赏雨后新晴的景致。黄蜂不断地扑向秋千上的绳索，是不是因这绳上还留有你当时手上的芳香。而令人怅惘的是，你的足迹再也回不到园中，那幽寂的台阶上，一夜之间长满了青苔。

【解析】

　　这首词乃伤春及怀人之作。上片写清明时分，又值风雨交加的天气，故而"愁"上心头。绿柳成荫，"晓梦啼莺"，更是徒增词人的寂寞。下片写故地重游，然而斯人不至，只有碧苔陡生。全词风格质朴淡雅，然而回忆与现实交织，情真意切。

47. "Wind through Pines" (Hearing the wind and rain, I pass the Clear and Bright Festival) by Wu Wenying

Hearing the wind and rain, I pass the Clear and Bright Festival. In melancholy, I draft an elegy on flowers. The green before the towers dim the road where we parted. One twig of willow, and one inch of tender affection. In chilly spring, I soak myself in wine. The oriole chirps startle my morning dream.

In the west garden, I clean day after day the woods pavilion. I still enjoy the new fine day. The wasps frequently alight on the chains of the swing, because the fragrance of her slender hands is still there. I feel depressed, for her foot traces are not present. Moss covers the quiet steps overnight.

【 Commentary 】

This lyric writes about the poet's sad feelings for the passage of spring and longings for his beloved. The Clear and bright Festival is mentioned in the first stanza, and the wild weather naturally evokes "sorrows" from the poet. The lines of green willows, the morning dream and the crying oriole add a sense of solitary. In the second stanza, he revisited an old haunt, but his beloved is not present and the green moss covers the steps overnight. With memories and realities intertwined, the style of the whole lyric is plain, graceful and sincere.

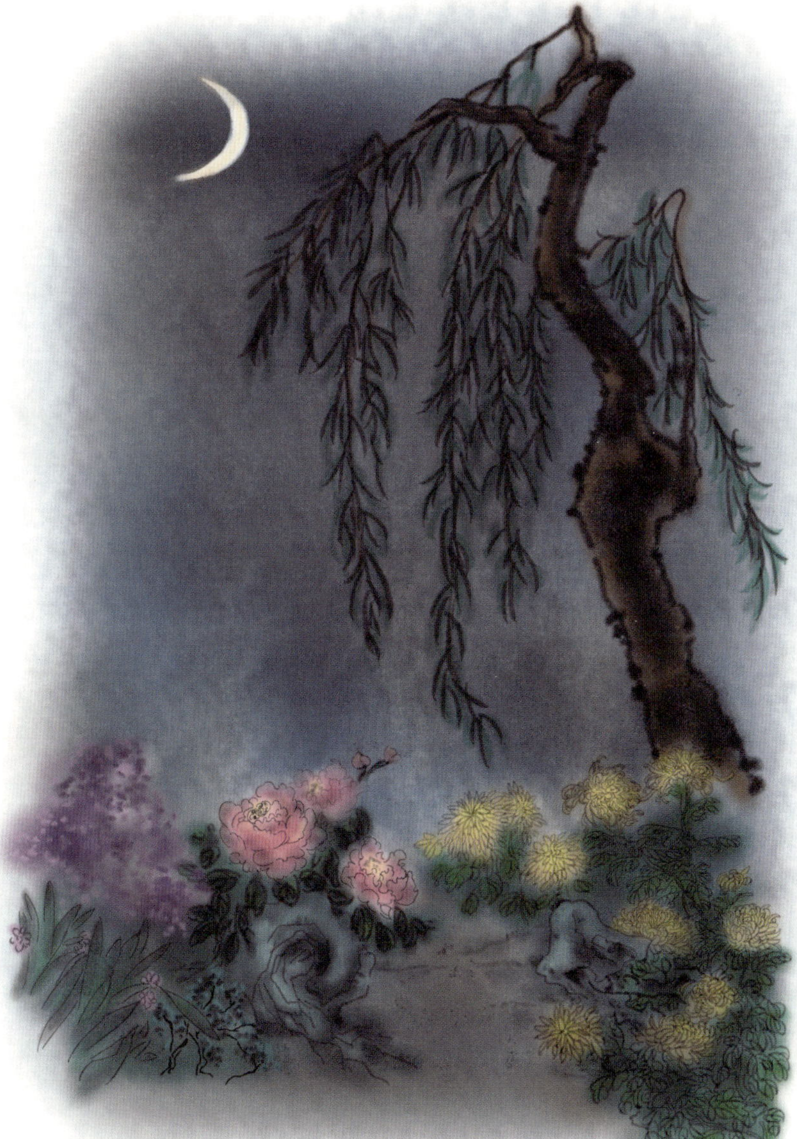

48. 王沂孙《眉妩·渐新痕悬柳》
新月

【原文】

渐新痕悬柳，淡彩穿花，依约破初暝。便有团圆意，深深拜，相逢谁在香径。画眉未稳，料素娥、犹带离恨。最堪爱、一曲银钩小，宝帘挂秋冷。

千古盈亏休问。叹慢磨玉斧，难补金镜。太液池犹在，凄凉处、何人重赋清景。故山夜永，试待他、窥户端正。看云外山河，还老尽、桂花影。

【释文】

一弯新月渐渐地升上来，似悬挂在柳树梢头，它那淡淡的月华穿过花丛，隐约像是把黑暗的天空划破了一条线。纵然这月儿已有团圆的端倪和迹象，然而那深深拜月的人，又有谁与她在花园小径中相逢（圆她团圆之愿）呢？此弯新月正如那纤细的眉毛没有画好，料想月中的嫦娥也还带着憾恨。最令人怜爱的是新月，如一弯小小的银钩，将窗帘似的天幕挂在清冷的秋夜里。

月儿的盈亏圆缺，千古以来都是如此，这其中的道理不必去细问。可叹的是徒然将玉斧磨快，也难以将残月修补好。太液池仍然在，而那景象如此凄凉，又有谁像当年的卢生一样，来重新对月赋

48. "Lovely Eyebrows" (Gradually the new moon hangs over the willow trees)
by Wang Yisun
New Moon

Gradually the new moon hangs over the willow trees. Its pale beams penetrate the flowers, as if they were breaking the twilight. It tends to turn full, and while bowing to it, whom shall I encounter on fragrant paths? It is like a tinted brow that is undulating, and perhaps the Moon Goddess still attaches to parting sorrows. What is most desirable is a small crooked silver hook that hangs over the pearl curtain of cold autumn.

Do not ask about its wax and wane across thousands of generations. I sigh that even if you slowly whet the jade axe, it is hard to mend the gold mirror. The Grand Liquid Pond remains there, but it is so desolate, and who would again praise the clear scene? The night of the old mountain is eternal, and I will wait until the moon peeps into the room and becomes full. See the mountains and rivers beyond the clouds, with an old age and in osmanthus shadows.

诗，歌咏清景。故国的河山，夜深且长。且等到来日月圆、清光照进窗户之时，斯人已老，再看那辽阔的河山，只能是在月影中。

【解析】

  这首词乃作者借新月来抒发山河破碎的遗民之恨。词的上片以写新月来寄托团圆之盼；下片上升到哲理的高度，借新月来叹人生的盈亏圆缺，从而写出国破家亡之后，百姓心中的哀痛以及他们渴望团聚的殷切心情。

【 Commentary 】

　　The poet employs the image of the new moon to express his grief as a loyalist of the previous dynasty. The first half writes about the new moon and the poet's expectation for reunion. The second half presents a philosophical sense of human life, because he likens the wane and wax of the moon to the reunions and separations as well as the unity and division in the mundane world. When a nation falls and a family is broken up, the commoners feel sorrowful and all they desire for is the unity of a nation and reunion of family members.

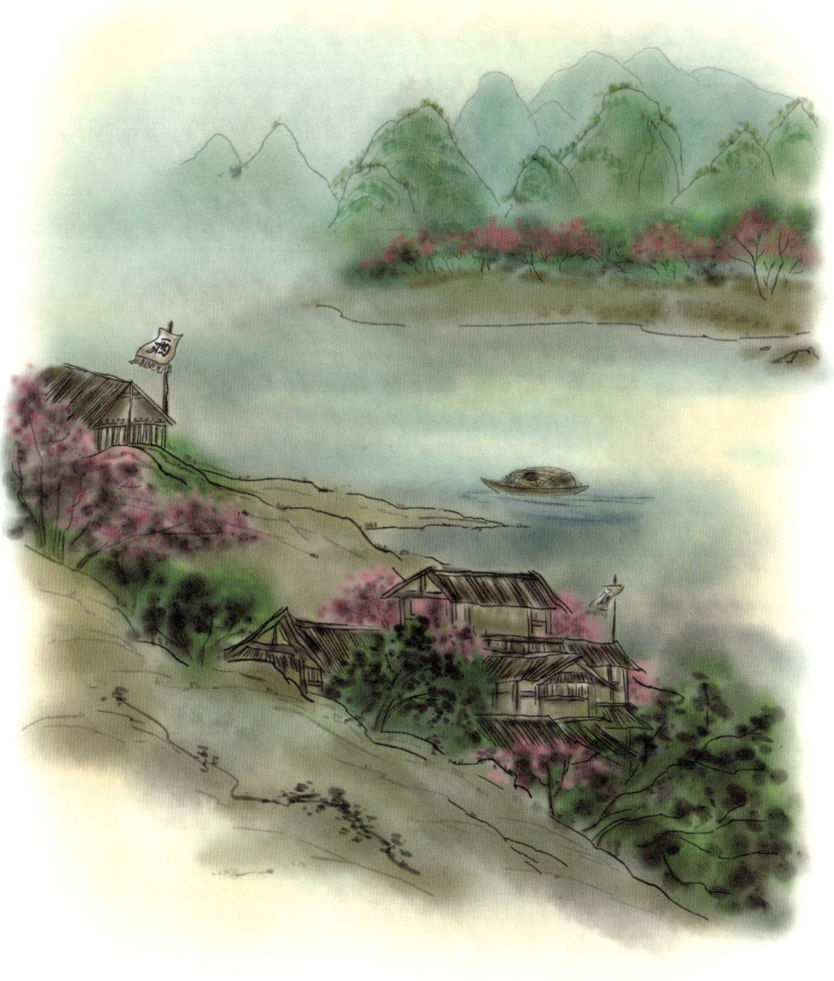
酒

49. 蒋捷《一剪梅·一片春愁待酒浇》
舟过吴江

【原文】

　　一片春愁待酒浇，江上舟摇，楼上帘招。秋娘渡与泰娘桥，风又飘飘，雨又萧萧。

　　何日归家洗客袍？银字笙调，心字香烧。流光容易把人抛，红了樱桃，绿了芭蕉。

【释文】

　　一片羁旅的春天的愁绪正等待借酒来消除，而此时的小舟在吴江上飘摇，江边岸上的酒旗飘飘，在招引着往来游客。哎，眼前便是秋娘渡与泰娘桥这样的美景，也无心欣赏，只感受到一片风雨潇潇。

　　何时才能回到家中？洗净旅途中沾满风霜的衣袍，调弄以银作字的笙，焚烧以心作形的香。流逝的时光使人有被抛弃之感，樱桃才红，芭蕉又绿了（春天已在不觉中远去）。

【解析】

　　这首词描述词人的伤春及羁旅之愁，而这些愁绪的根本则在于由乱离所带来的归家无望。"红了樱桃，绿了芭蕉"二句为历来传诵的名句，借这一"红"一"绿"两种可感知的色调，将时光的易逝形象地表现出来。

49. "A Twig of Mume Blossoms" (The boundless spring grief awaits the pouring of the wine) by Jiang Jie
The Boat Passes Wu River

The boundless spring grief awaits the pouring of the wine, rowing boats on the river and flying streamers on wine towers. Around Autumn Maid Ferry and Tai Maid Bridge, wind blows strongly and rain falls rapidly.

What day can I return home to wash my traveler's robe? To play on silver lute and burn the heart-shaped incense. Time is fleeting, and leaves everyone behind. While cherries just turn red, bananas become green.

【 Commentary 】

This song conveys the poet's sorrows for the passage of spring and nostalgia, all of which are brought by a chaotic time that leads to his hopelessness in returning home. The last couplet has been fairly popular since the song was written. The fresh colors "red" and "green" vividly show how fast time flies!

南開大學出版社

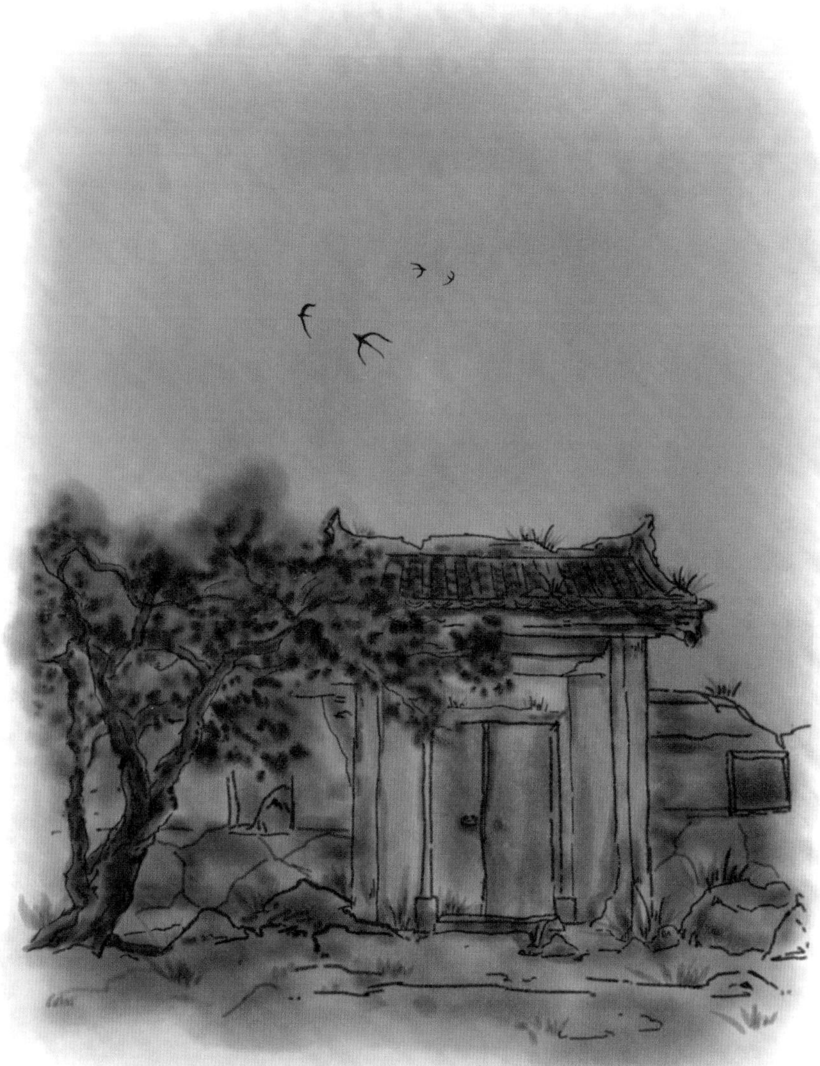

50. 张炎《高阳台·接叶巢莺》
西湖春感

【原文】

接叶巢莺,平波卷絮,断桥斜日归船。能几番游?看花又是明年。东风且伴蔷薇住,到蔷薇、春已堪怜。更凄然,万绿西泠,一抹荒烟。

当年燕子知何处?但苔深韦曲,草暗斜川。见说新愁,如今也到鸥边。无心再续笙歌梦,掩重门、浅醉闲眠。莫开帘,怕见飞花,怕听啼鹃。

【释文】

茂密的树叶中有黄莺筑巢,泛起的水波卷起了飘落的柳絮,斜阳照着经过断桥回到城里去的船。这样的游赏一年中能有几次呢?再等到看花之时,又得到明年了。东风啊,还是暂且与蔷薇为伴,少驻片刻,因为蔷薇花开之时,春天已到值得怜惜的地步了。更令人凄恻的是,浓绿掩映的西泠桥,也只能看见一抹荒凉的烟霭了。

当年栖息在豪门大户的燕子不知道现在飞向了何处。只见那些富户旧居长满了青苔,文人游赏胜地也因荒草疯长而被遮暗。听说那沙鸥也感染了新近传来的忧愁。至于我,也无心再继续从前笙歌游乐的梦,只是将那一道道的门关上,稍稍喝点酒,悠闲地睡一会儿。请不要将帘幕打开,我怕看到落花纷飞,也怕听到杜鹃悲鸣。

50. "High Sun Terrace" (Orioles nest in leaves that are closely joined) by Zhang Yan
Thoughts on Spring on West Lake

Orioles nest in leaves that are closely joined; waves roll up the catkins on the lake surface. The Broken Bridge, the slanting sun and the returning boats. How many tours can there be? To appreciate flowers, wait till next year. The eastern wind, please just stay with the roses, when roses are blooming, it will be the late spring, and how pitiful! What is more pitiful, the Xiling bridge with myriads of layers of greenness, will be seen in a touch of desolate mist.

Who knows where the swallows in those years fly? One could only see that the moss grows deep in Weiqu, and Xiechuan becomes dim due to the overgrowth of the grass. I hear that the new sorrows have now reached the gulls. In no mood to continue the dream of the pipe songs. Close layers of doors, drinking a few cups of wine and taking a nap leisurely. Do not pull the curtain open, I am afraid of seeing flying flowers, and hearing chirps of cuckoos.

【解析】

  杭州作为南宋偏安时的京都，本是极繁华热闹之地，然而随着南宋日趋衰亡，杭州也渐萧条。诗人于春日来临之际，泛舟西湖这个杭州有名的风景胜地时，感受到的尽是繁华逝去的荒芜。"怕见飞花，怕听啼鹃"更是写出了诗人的亡国哀痛之情。

【 Commentary 】

As the capital of the Southern Song dynasty, Hangzhou city should have been a prosperous place. But when the dynasty came to an end, Hangzhou gradually became desolate. When spring was approaching, the poet came to the West Lake on a boat, but all he saw was a scene of desolation. The last couplet indirectly describes the sad feelings of the poet for the subjugation of the nation.

翻译后记

诗歌，乃翻译中失去的东西。常常翻译诗歌的人应该不太会反对这种说法。以中国诗歌中的某些意象为例，如"西窗""西楼""西风""西山""西厢"等，虽然它们很容易按照字面意思被转译为外国文字，但外国读者若不了解其蕴藏在深层的传统文化内涵，以及与历史名人或历代名篇的某种对话与互文关系，那么便不容易充分理解并体会到诗歌中的文字美和意境美。因此，翻译的确会使诗歌丧失一些原有的东西。但同样也有人认为，诗歌，乃翻译中得到的东西。翻译诗歌时，源语言本身的音韵、节奏和律动等特点很难在"功能对等"层面上以译入语的形式再现。但译者也可以选择通过对文本进行自由阐释和"再创作"的方式在译文中重构新的"韵脚"，这也能在一定程度上解决译诗押韵的问题。然而正如奚如谷（Stephen H. West, 1944— ）教授指出的那样，"直译"或许有诸多不尽如人意之处，但是通过"诉诸英语中的陈词滥调来简化那些对读者积极介入会带来挑战的段落，既无必要，也不可取"。（The Story of the Western Wing, 1995, p.15）

事实上，没有任何一种文学翻译的方法，在理论和实践层面上都是绝对完美无瑕的，但好的译者可以尽最大可能地通过译文来帮助读者去接近古人在阅读原文时的感受与经验。我深信，想要真正体味中国诗词歌赋的美，最理想的办法莫过于直接去学习汉语本身。

在此，我要感谢导师奚如谷教授多年来的悉心教导，是他教会了我如何进行文学翻译，他常常告诉我，翻译并不是阐释，不要低估或主观臆断读者对于文字本身的感悟力、解析力、想象力和鉴赏力。在翻译本选集时，笔者参考了杨宪益先生、许渊冲先生等前辈大家的英译宋词作品，获益匪浅，笔者特向以上诸位学者和教授表示诚挚的感谢和深深的敬意！同时要十分感谢广西师范大学出版社虞劲松老师、王专老师、梁鑫磊老师、梁嗣辰老师、尤晓澍老师及其他匿名译审老师！没有他们的信任、支持、和指导，这本译作是无法完成的。对于译文中仍存在的衍误和不妥之处，译者本人负全部责任。

吴思远

2023 年 2 月 22 日华盛顿贝灵汉

Postscript

Translators of poems usually agree that "poetry is what gets lost in translation." Some images in Chinese poetry, such as "western window," "western tower," "western wind," "western mountains," and "western wing," etc., can be easily translated into a foreign language. Yet, foreign readers may not easily and sufficiently perceive the literary and the aesthetic beauty of a poem, if they do not understand the cultural meanings embodies in certain words or phrases, or if they ignore an intertextual relationship between some borrowed lines and the well-known verses. Therefore, it is not unreasonable that a poem does lose something in its translation. There are those who also believe that "poetry is what is gained in translation." It is indeed difficult to find the functional equivalents for some poetic lines featured by rhymes and rhythms. Still, translators could choose to present a paraphrase version of the original texts and "reproduce" the rhymed verses in target language. Admittedly, literal translation, to some extent, might not be unproblematic, but as Professor Stephen West pointed out, "it is both unnecessary and undesirable to resort to well-worn English equivalents or clichés to smooth over any passages that challenge the reader to active engagement" (The Story of the Western Wing, 1995, p.15). As a matter of fact, either in theory or in practice, there is no such thing as an absolutely perfect method for literary translation. However, a good translator of ancient poems will render a foreign version through which the modern readers may experience to the utmost extent what the ancient readers felt when they read the original texts. I personally believe that perhaps the ideal way to get a real taste of Chinese poems, songs and rhapsodies is to study Chinese language.

I want to, first and foremost, thank my adviser and mentor Professor Stephen H. West for his years of guidance, support and encouragement. He teaches me to know what literary translation is. He also convinces me of the fact that it is more significant to translate what the texts say than to translate what the texts mean, and that we should never underestimate readers' ability to apprehend, analyze, imagine and appreciate what they read. I also give my thanks and respects to Mr. Yang Xianyi and Mr. Xu Yuanchong, whose translation works provide me with references. Last but not least, I would like to express my sincere gratitude to the editors of Guangxi Normal University Press: Mr. Yu Jinsong, Ms. Shi Ping, Ms. Wang Zhuan, Mr. Liang Xinlei, Mr. Liang Sichen, Ms. You Xiaoshu and the anonymous proofreader. This book could not be completed without their trust, support and suggestions. For any errors remain in this book, I take complete responsibility for them.

Wu Siyuan
February 22, 2023 Bellingham, Washington